MR. WONDERFUL

The lights dimmed, and romantic music filled the room. Dave *was* the most impressive date any girl could ask for. Sara knew she had gotten her wish. It would be a night she would always remember. But maybe not for the reason she'd expected. Out of the corner of her eye she could see Chris dancing cheek to cheek with Jennifer. She couldn't tear her gaze away, any more than she could dismiss the feeling for Chris that was blossoming inside her.

Bantam Sweet Dreams Romances
Ask your bookseller for the books you have missed

Mr. Wonderful

Fran Michaels

BANTAM BOOKS

TORONTO · NEW YORK · LONDON · SYDNEY · AUCKLAND

RL 6, IL age 11 and up

MR. WONDERFUL

A Bantam Book / July 1987

ISBN 0-553-26340-4

Published simultaneously in the United States and Canada

*Bantam Books are published by Bantam Books, Inc. Its trademark,
consisting of the words "Bantam Books" and the portrayal of
a rooster, is Registered in U.S. Patent and Trademark Office
and in other countries. Marca Registrada. Bantam Books, Inc.,
666 Fifth Avenue, New York, New York 10103.*

*Reproduced, printed and bound in Great Britain by
Hazell Watson & Viney Limited,
Member of the BPCC Group,
Aylesbury, Bucks*

Dedicated to Mike, Danny, Scott, Mom and Dad, all of whom never stopped believing.

Chapter One

"If I see one more little black bat, I'm going to scream," threatened Katie Wilcox as she placed her latest creation on top of a huge pile of Halloween cutouts.

"And if I have to draw one more ugly wart on one more witch's nose, I might join you," said Marsha Gregory. Emphatically she snapped the cap back on her black felt-tip marker and stretched her arms up.

"What do you guys have to complain about? At least you have dates for the dance," said Sara Grant. She bent over the art table, intently sketching a huge, smiling jack-o'-lantern, a jumble of medium-length
falling forward.

"You'd have a date, too, if you weren't so stubborn," said Katie, her eyebrows knitting together in exasperation. "I really wish you'd let me fix you up with Jason's cousin. Jason says he's a terrific guy, and it sure beats sitting home on Halloween night while the rest of Stanford High is at the dance."

Sara shook her head, her usually gentle face set determinedly. "I can still remember the last date you and Jason arranged for me, and I promised myself then I'd *never* go on a blind date again," she said firmly. "Never."

"Not all blind dates are awful," said Marsha diplomatically.

"Well, *I* think it's awful to have to go out with somebody one minute after you've met him, whether you like him or not," said Sara.

"You never did tell us the gory details of your date with Joel," said Katie. She leaned her elbows on the long wooden table and looked at her friend expectantly.

Sara tilted her head to the side. "It wasn't really Joel's fault, I guess. It's just that we had absolutely nothing in common. He had tickets for us to go to a basketball game at Madison Square Garden. Basically he lives and breathes basketball—he knew the names of every player on *both* teams!"

"What's wrong with that?" Marsha shrugged.

"Nothing, except, as you know, I don't even know the rules of the game, much less any statistics," she said ruefully. Katie laughed. "When we left the Garden," continued Sara, "we stopped for ice cream before taking the train home to Connecticut. But all Joel could do was talk about basketball in the ice-cream parlor and on the train. It didn't take us long to realize that we weren't exactly made for each other."

"I think you should have just asked him to explain the game to you," Katie said reasonably.

"He did, but to tell you the truth, I was bored," admitted Sara. "I thought that we could talk about something that interested me, so I mentioned how much I loved old movies. You know, like *It Happened One Night* with Clark Gable and Claudette Colbert." Sara sighed, a smile stealing across her face.

Marsha nodded enthusiastically. "That's a classic—I love it, too. What did Joel say to that?"

"Well, not only doesn't he like old movies, but he went so far as to say he couldn't understand how *anybody* could bear to watch them. He thinks today's movies have the old duds from the thirties and forties beat by a mile." Sara looked pointedly at Katie.

"Sara, sometimes you just have to pretend to share a boy's interests," said Katie. "It's all kind of like playing a game."

"Now you sound like my mother!" Sara tossed her dark hair. "Sometimes I think she really believes a woman's only purpose is to be a loyal and good wife."

"Well, I wouldn't go *that* far." Katie smiled. "But I still think there's a grain of truth in her theory."

"Well, I can't tell where my dad ends and my mom begins." Sara shook her head emphatically.

"Don't knock it. As long as it works for your parents, that's all that matters," said Katie. "Look at how many people get divorced these days."

"I suppose so. It's just that my mom doesn't seem to have a life of her own. Besides being his wife, she works for my dad as his dental nurse and secretary, too. I don't know how she has enough minutes in the day left to breathe," Sara mused.

"She's happy, isn't she?" asked Katie, her blue eyes wide and serious.

Sara nodded. "Yes, she really is. But I don't think I could ever be that way."

She glanced mischievously at her friends, then picked up a brightly colored cardboard

4

witch and sent it sailing across the art room just as the bell rang, signaling the end of the period. Marsha and Katie giggled. Sara pushed back her chair and stashed her art materials in the cubbyhole.

"Hey, why don't we hang one of your pumpkins out in the hall right now?" suggested Marsha, shuffling through the pile of drawings.

"I beg your pardon," Sara corrected her haughtily. "These are not *pumpkins*, they are *jack-o'-lanterns*."

"Oh, I'm so sorry," said Marsha in a high-pitched English accent.

"We have to hurry." Sara grabbed a package of tacks. "Mr. Josephson will tar and feather me if I'm late for English. He takes it personally when a student walks in five seconds after the final bell, as though he's worried Shakespeare might be rolling over in his grave at the insult."

The girls hurried out into the hall to the long cork bulletin board that ran the length of the wall outside the art room.

"I really hope these dumb decorations get kids in the Halloween mood," Katie said as she helped Sara center a toothless orange face next to a poster advertising the dance.

"You know, that *does* look pretty good, if I say so myself!" Sara pushed three tacks into the jack-o'-lantern and smiled with satisfaction, then stepped back from the board to admire her artwork.

"It sure does," agreed a deep male voice.

Sara whirled around and found herself staring into the clearest and most beautiful ocean blue eyes she had ever seen. They were literally only inches away. She gasped in surprise and took a step backward, quite a feat considering the fact that her knees had just turned to rubber.

She had had a secret crush on David Reiner since her eighth-grade Spanish class. He had sat next to her, and he was a terrible student. It was a miracle that she had learned anything herself, since she had spent most of the time sneaking glances at his gorgeous profile.

Dave smiled a devastating movie-star smile. His dimples made Sara's heart lurch crazily.

"Did you really draw that?" he asked, stepping closer to study the jack-o'-lantern.

Sara nodded, speechless. She was mesmerized by the waves in Dave's thick black hair. "Uh, yes," she finally stammered. She felt like a silly freshman instead of a mature junior.

"It's terrific. I can't even draw a straight line." He smiled and winked at Sara.

"But you can write—those great articles in

6

the school paper," said Sara. She never missed reading one of David's articles in the Stanford *Star.*

"You like them?" Dave was obviously pleased with the compliment. "I'm doing one now on the Halloween Costume Dance—just like your drawing."

Sara's heart thumped loudly in her chest—it sounded to her as if it would explode.

"I'm on the decorating committee. We're hanging these all over the school. Later we'll be transforming the gym into a haunted house," she said casually, trying not to look too amazed that Dave Reiner was actually standing there having a conversation with her.

Dave nodded. His smile faded for a second, and then it was back brighter than ever. He looked into Sara's huge blue eyes as if he were seeing her for the first time.

"Sara Grant, right?" he asked.

She nodded, surprised that he knew her name.

"Haven't we had some classes together?"

"English last year, and Spanish in eighth grade," Sara said, twisting a curl nervously around her finger.

Dave's eyes lit up with recognition. "I remember you now! You were the girl who never scored under ninety-eight on any Spanish test." He shook his head ruefully. "I really used to struggle in that class. Spanish still drives me crazy."

"It's really not that hard. Just a lot of memorization. All those verb tenses, you know." You're making captivating conversation, Sara Grant, she chided herself. It's the first real encounter you've ever had with David Reiner, and all you can talk about is Spanish! I bet the other girls Dave talks to have a lot more interesting things to say.

Dave raised an eyebrow skeptically. "Well, maybe there's hope for me yet. Hey, I remember you offered to tutor me back in eighth grade. Does the offer still stand, by any chance?" he asked hopefully.

Sara wasn't sure whether he was joking or not, so she decided it would be safer not to say anything at all. She just smiled encouragingly instead.

"How about going to a movie on Saturday night?" Dave said, suddenly changing the subject. "That'll give you some time to consider my proposition."

Sara was too shocked to notice that Dave had flushed slightly when he suggested the movie. She couldn't believe this was actually happening to her—she was bound to wake up and find out it was just a dream.

"What do you say?" Dave ran a hand briskly through his hair.

"Sure, I'd love to." Sara jumped as the first bell signaling the start of the next period echoed loudly in the empty hallway.

"Got to run! I'll pick you up at seven-thirty," he called over his shoulder as he sprinted down the long corridor, his denim jacket sailing out behind him. Then suddenly he stopped and turned back to Sara. "Where do you live?" he called.

"Eighty-five Willow Lane," Sara answered, feeling a little foolish. She felt as though everyone in the school was listening as her voice echoed down the hall.

Dave nodded and turned, running to his class. Sara stood rooted to the spot. She had forgotten about Mr. Josephson, English, Shakespeare, and academic responsibility. The only thought that kept repeating in her mind was that David Reiner had asked her out on a date for Saturday night. She shook her head at the jack-o'-lantern, mystified. It grinned back at her.

"Beware of boys on the rebound," warned Katie. She sat cross-legged on Sara's brass

9

bed, watching her friend ransack her closet in search of the perfect outfit for her date that night.

"What do you mean by that?" demanded Sara.

"Just that Dave broke up with Julie Redman over the summer, and he may not be over her yet. He has quite a reputation with girls at school, too, you know." Katie leaned back on her elbows, her shoulder-length blond hair falling on the pillow.

"I don't want to hear about any of that," Sara insisted, closing her mind to pictures of Dave with the beautiful redheaded Julie.

"Before he went out with Julie he dated Heather Shearer, and Nicole Talbot before her," Katie ticked the names off on her fingers. "I think Dave's gone out with the whole cheerleading squad!"

"Well, as far as I'm concerned, Dave and Julie aren't together anymore, and I don't care about the rest of those girls. All that matters to me is that he asked *me* out. I never *dreamed* he would." Sara tossed a blue turtleneck sweater aside and dove back into the closet.

"Why not? What are you, a leper?" Katie made a face at her friend's back. "You just don't have enough self-confidence," she observed solemnly.

Sara stopped her frantic search for a moment and turned to face Katie. "Dave's special," she said quietly. "I've never known anyone like him before."

"Sara, don't put him on a pedestal," advised Katie. "He's just a guy, like Jason and a million others. Well, maybe not like Jason," she amended with a smile, referring to her boyfriend. "But he *is* only human. The only thing that makes him different is that he's fantastic looking, and he knows it."

"That's why you've got to help me find something to wear that'll blow him away," pleaded Sara, ignoring her friend's warning.

Katie was a genius with clothes and could put together a terrific outfit from anything.

"OK," said Katie, bouncing off the bed to stand beside Sara who was peering into her closet. "Here," she suggested, lifting out a soft red snowflake sweater and holding it against her own slender body. "This will look great with your new white knit stirrup pants."

Sara tilted her head to the side, considering the combination. Grinning happily, she gave her friend a bear hug, and waltzed her around the pretty lavender-and-white bedroom.

"What would I do without you, Katie? You're

incredible!" Sara giggled and then was suddenly serious again. "Do you think he'll like my hair?" She peered into the full-length mirror that hung on her closet door, her face pinched with worry.

"Sara, you've really lost your mind." Katie placed her hands on her hips in mock exasperation. "I bet Princess Di didn't go to this much trouble before her first date with Prince Charles!"

"But it's so wild and bushy," complained Sara, gathering her hair in her hands and pushing it on top of her head.

"You have the thickest, most gorgeous hair I've ever seen. Anyone would kill for your curls," Katie teased.

Sara couldn't help giggling.

"Here, why don't you try tying this up in your hair?" Katie lifted a bright red chiffon scarf from Sara's dresser drawer.

Sara stood still while Katie tied the scarf loosely around her head in an off-center bow, fluffing her dark curls out around the soft material. Sara cocked her head reflectively to the side, and smiled at the result. "It *does* look kind of nice," she admitted.

"It looks terrific," said Katie emphatically. "And now Dave'll wonder why he never asked you out before."

Sara laughed, unable to contain the happiness bubbling inside her. "You're a true friend, Katie Wilcox," she said. "Maybe I'll get to the Halloween dance after all! Wouldn't that be wonderful?" she said, her face aglow.

"That's a possibility." Katie nodded prophetically. "A definite possibility."

Chapter Two

Sara spread her fingers out on the glass top of her dressing table. She should never have let Katie talk her into wearing bright red nail polish. It just wasn't her style, not that she even knew what her style *was*.

Katie loved wearing bright colors. That was just the way she was; she always made a splash—people *noticed* her. She'd been the star of the sophomore school play and would probably play the lead in the junior show that year. She knew what clothes to wear, and she could fix her hair in at least two dozen gorgeous styles. If Sara hadn't known her since kindergarten, she wasn't sure what they would have in common now. But the fact was that she and Katie were the best of friends.

"You've got to spice up your image," Katie always insisted. "Come out of your shell, and don't be afraid to let guys get to know you."

Sara knew what her friend meant. She had a lot of *girl*friends, but boys didn't exactly flock around her. She knew it was probably because she felt shy and insecure around them. But she never knew what to say when she was with a guy, unlike Katie who could talk to anyone and not feel the least bit self-conscious.

Well, Sara decided, I certainly don't want to be my plain old dull self for this date with Dave. I've been given one chance—I can't blow it! After all, Dave's used to dating sophisticated girls like Julie Redman.

Sara grimaced at the thought of her glamorous classmate. Julie was one of the most popular girls at Stanford High and a real trend setter. She'd come to school one day wearing an oversize Mickey Mouse sweatshirt, and within a week, half the girls in the junior class were wearing sweatshirts emblazoned with cartoon characters from Betty Boop to Gumby.

Sara herself never idolized Julie and her other equally sophisticated friends. She would never be as popular as Julie, but at least she was her own person. And right then she was very pleased with what she saw as she pirouetted in front of her full-length mirror. The warm red knit sweater set off her dark complexion; and the white stretch pants made the most of her long, slim legs. Even her hair looked satisfactory for once. She adjusted the red scarf and batted her eyelashes at her reflection.

She glanced at her new plaid watch for the twentieth time. Seven-forty. Dave should have been there already. Actually he should have been there ten minutes before. But that's what dates were all about. The boy is late just to make sure the girl has lots of time to get *really* nervous.

Sara bounced on the edge of her bed. Abby, her gray-brown Great Dane, lay sprawled on the lavender-and-white coverlet, her massive head resting on the lace-edged pillows. She watched Sara sympathetically with her dark, drooping eyes. Sara knew that if her mom and dad came into the room they'd have a fit. They had forbidden Sara to let Abby onto the bed, but Abby refused to sleep on the floor. She didn't know that she was enormous; she seriously considered herself a lapdog. Sara had rescued Abby from the dog pound two

16

years before, and it had been love at first sight. Abby stuck to Sara's side like a grateful shadow, and Sara confided all of her problems to the dog. She never had to worry about sounding silly—Abby always understood.

"Well, Abster, what do you think?" Sara stroked the Great Dane's soft black nose. "Am I being stood up?" Abby didn't even open her eyes. Sara laughed. "No cause for alarm, huh?"

Suddenly Abby's ears perked up, and the rest of her body followed. She galloped to the window and placed paws the size of baseball mitts on the sill, barking for all she was worth. Sara heard a car door slam, and then the doorbell rang. She heard her mother open the door.

Her hands suddenly went as cold and clammy as Abby's nose. "Here goes nothing, dog."

Sara turned the doorknob, and Abby pushed out ahead of her, anxious to greet the newcomer. The Great Dane made it down the stairs in one leap with Sara following in her wake. Then, to Sara's horror, Abby reared back and stood on her hind legs, putting her front paws on Dave's shoulders and washing his face with dog kisses.

"What the?" Dave staggered backward from the impact of one hundred and fifty pounds of Abby.

"Abby!" cried Sara, running forward to pull the dog off Dave. Reluctantly, Abby let herself be led away by Mrs. Grant.

"I'm so sorry, Dave. Abby just loves company, and she doesn't know her own strength." What an embarrassing way to start off her first date with Dave! It would probably be her last now, Sara thought. She was mortified, but at the same time she had to fight off an almost irresistible urge to giggle.

"That's OK," said Dave, brushing off his brown leather jacket and smiling weakly. "I was prepared to shake hands with your father, but I certainly didn't expect *that*."

"She's just a big, overgrown puppy." The giggle burst out of Sara, despite herself.

"Some puppy!" Dave shook his head and glanced into the hallway mirror, smoothing his hair back into place with his fingers.

"Abby's safely locked in the kitchen," said Mrs. Grant, walking back into the front hall. "I hope she didn't ruin your clothes, Dave."

"No, I'm fine." Dave seemed to have recovered himself. He gave Mrs. Grant one of his traffic-stopping smiles.

"Well, I'd like to say she doesn't usually behave that way, but the truth is that she does. Sara spoils her rotten."

Sara blushed. She caught her mother's eye

and wrinkled her forehead fiercely. When Dave bent over to tie his shoe, she mouthed, "Change the subject, Mom! Enough about the dog!"

"What movie are you going to see?" Mrs. Grant asked helpfully. Sara reached into the closet for her khaki poplin jacket.

"There are three new ones playing at the Cinema Triplex in town. I thought I'd let Sara choose when we get there."

Dave held Sara's jacket so she could slip her arms into the sleeves more easily. She turned to smile at him. He was really thoughtful. He handled everything like a gentleman. Maybe this date wasn't getting off to such a bad start after all.

"Well, let me know what's playing, Sara. Maybe I can get your father to take me sometime soon," said Mrs. Grant.

"Where *is* Daddy?" asked Sara. Her father always made a point of meeting her friends, whether they were girls or the few boys she had dated.

"I'm afraid he had a meeting, but I'm sure he'll meet you the next time, David."

Sara cringed inside. Wouldn't you know? Just when she thought her parents were through embarrassing her in front of one of her friends, they'd say something like that.

How could her mother just assume that there would even *be* a next time?

David didn't seem to notice her mother's remark. "I'd like that." He smiled as he reached for the door. "We won't be back too late," he promised, placing his hand on Sara's back as he stepped out after her. Mrs. Grant called goodbye as the door closed behind them.

The gentle pressure of Dave's hand caused an electric shock to zip through Sara's body. She was nervous and excited all at the same time. Half of her wanted to take one giant step away from him, the other half wanted to stay close by.

In the driveway, Dave held open the passenger door to his fire engine-red Camaro. Sara slid into the seat, running her hands over the smooth upholstery. The spicy scent of Dave's cologne mingled with the crisp October smell of fallen leaves. Sara knew the aroma would always remind her of their first date. *Our first date, and please, not our last!* She shivered.

"Cold?"

Sara nodded. She couldn't exactly tell him that it was being so close to him, not the cold, windy night, that gave her goose bumps.

"Come over here," he said. He put a strong

20

arm around her shoulders and pulled her close to him.

Sara realized that she was holding her breath, and she let it out slowly and shakily. Being with Dave like that made her feel breathless and light-headed. He'd never even spoken to her until just a few days before, and now he was sitting so close beside her that she could feel the warmth of his body against her side.

"Feel any warmer?" he asked, his lips next to her ear.

"Yes, I'm fine," she answered, wishing she could think of something interesting to say. But Dave's presence—all six foot one of him— did away with whatever conversation-making abilities she possessed.

"Good," said David in a low voice. No one had ever spoken to Sara in a sexy tone, but if that wasn't one she didn't know what was. A shiver ran up her spine. "I knew I could warm you up. Do you like Camaros?" He changed the subject abruptly.

Sara didn't want to admit that she wouldn't know a Camaro from a Cadillac. "Your car is beautiful," she said, mesmerized by the bright dashboard. It looked like the control panel of a spaceship—everything was digital and clearly state-of-the-art. Sara's family's comfortable

Buick and the little orange Toyota she owned belonged to another species altogether.

"Thanks." David was obviously pleased with the compliment. "I've only had it for two months," he said proudly. "Want to hear a stereo system that'll blow your mind?" He pushed a Bruce Springsteen tape into the cassette player.

Dave pulled out of the Grants' driveway with music blaring from all four speakers. He adjusted the controls every few seconds and sang along with the music. He was so involved that Sara wouldn't have been surprised if he had let go of the steering wheel to join Bruce Springsteen for a guitar jam. One thing was clear—he seemed to have forgotten that Sara was in the car until they had almost reached the movie theater.

"I love Springsteen," he said with a grin as the tape ended.

"Me, too," agreed Sara. It was true, but she couldn't help thinking that Dave might have paid a little less attention to his stereo and a little more to his date.

"Would you like to try driving this baby sometime?" Dave patted the dashboard, watching carefully to see her reaction to his offer.

Sara's blue eyes opened wide in surprise.

Any flicker of disappointment she might have felt dissolved instantly. Dave was even more wonderful than she had imagined! What other guy would let a girl drive his brand-new sports car?

"I'd love to, but I'd be afraid something might happen to it," she said shyly.

"Don't be silly." Dave waved her worry aside. "I'd be right beside you," he promised. "And I'm a great driver. My dad used to let me practice in our driveway when I was only fourteen, and I got my license as soon as I turned sixteen."

Sara nodded. "I got my license as soon as I could, too."

"Well, here's the theater," said Dave, pulling into a parking space. "And look at those lines!"

"I'm sure we'll get seats," Sara said hopefully. Dave took her hand and pulled her along beside him as he hurried toward the theater.

"I think you're right, Sara," he said with a sudden smile. "We'll get seats all right." Sara followed Dave's glance to the front of the line where a boy and a girl were waving to them eagerly.

"You guys are a sight for sore eyes," said Dave, slapping the other boy on the back in a hearty greeting. Sara recognized Chuck Taylor. His picture was always in the sports section of the school paper for one sport or another, most recently for scoring an incredible touchdown.

His girlfriend, Anita Marcus, was pretty and popular—and a very good friend of Julie Redman.

"Hi, Davey," crooned Anita, smiling warmly at him.

Dave returned the smile, flashing his dimples. It was clear to Sara that the other girl was affected by Dave's good looks, but she had to admit that it was impossible not to be. *She* melted whenever Dave turned his brilliant smile on her—so she could hardly blame Anita. Still . . .

"You don't mind if we sneak into the line here, do you?" Dave spoke with assurance—it was a statement, not a question.

He turned to Sara. "It's OK, if we see the spy flick, isn't it?" He squeezed her hand. "It's gotten great reviews, and by the time we wait in any of the other lines here, the shows will be sold out."

Sara hesitated for only a moment. It wouldn't have been her first choice, but Dave was right, they might not get in any of the others.

"This movie's fine," she agreed with a smile.

David rewarded her with a wide grin. "Boy,

am I glad we were reunited in that hallway," he said happily, slipping into line in front of his friends with Sara held tight by his side. They stepped up to the box office and bought their tickets, then were joined by Chuck and Anita in the lobby.

"Smooth move, buddy," Chuck said, laughing.

Sara was a little embarrassed by the irritated glances they were receiving from a few of the other moviegoers. She would never cut into a line like that herself, but somehow when Dave did it it seemed exciting and adventurous instead of rude.

"Hey, I'm sorry." Dave apologized as if he'd only just become aware of Sara's presence. "I forgot to introduce you guys. Sara, this is my good buddy, Chuck Taylor, and this gorgeous girl with him is Anita Marcus. Guys, this is Sara Grant, who is single-handedly decorating the school for Halloween."

Chuck smiled at Sara and nodded hello. Anita's smile was much cooler, and her appraising stare made Sara uncomfortable. She wondered if the other girl would report back to Julie. She bet the report wouldn't be favorable.

"I think Dave's exaggerating," Sara said.

"Oh, old Dave here doesn't exaggerate very

often," said Chuck. "I've seen some of the decorations, and they're really good," he said to Sara.

Sara wanted to explain that Marsha and Katie were equally responsible, but the other kids had turned their attention to the candy counter. She found herself starting to talk to an older couple standing next to her. She turned pink with embarrassment.

"Is a large buttered popcorn all right with you?" asked David, turning back toward Sara. She nodded in agreement.

She felt a wave of disappointment wash over her when Chuck and Anita rejoined them after buying their own popcorn and soda. She had wanted to have Dave all to herself for the evening, and now suddenly it looked as if they were on a double date.

"We are never going to find four seats together, because we stopped for popcorn first," Dave said as they headed down the crowded aisle. "We should have gotten seats first."

Chuck nodded. "Well, Anita and I'll sit back here. There are two seats farther down," he said, pointing toward the middle of the theater.

Dave took Sara's hand and ushered her toward the empty seats before someone else could claim them. "Alone at last," he whispered in her ear.

Sara looked up at him in surprise, not knowing whether he was teasing her or not. He looked perfectly serious, but a minute ago she would have thought he'd be happy to have the whole football team along on their date. Was it possible that he really wanted to be alone with her?

"Have some popcorn." Dave placed a kernal gently between her lips, his blue eyes holding hers intensely.

Sara was so surprised she almost choked. She chewed and swallowed the piece of popcorn self-consciously. Dave didn't take his eyes off her the entire time.

"You're so pretty, Sara," he whispered. It seemed as if it were taking place in slow motion to Sara as he moved his face closer to hers and she felt the warmth of his lips on hers. It was as if all the noise and people surrounding them had melted away and they were completely alone. It was magical.

Sara slowly drifted back to reality as the lights dimmed and the movie began. Dave released her and settled back in his seat, leaving his arm around her shoulders.

She had never liked spy movies—she liked the kind of movies that she could relax with, not ones that she had to concentrate on the plot every minute.

She had a particularly hard time concentrating on that one. She could still feel the pressure of Dave's lips on hers and was very conscious of his arm around her. Every once in a while he would pull her closer to him. She was sure the whole movie theater was illuminated by her burning cheeks.

She tried to follow the story line, knowing her mother would ask her about the movie in the morning. It was something about smugglers in Europe and C.I.A. agents—the usual. She could probably bluff it.

When the lights came on again, Dave stretched his arms to the ceiling. "That was terrific, wasn't it?" he asked, turning toward Sara.

She was just about to say, "It wasn't really my kind of movie," but she bit back the words. She didn't want a repeat of her blind date with Joel. She hadn't really cared about him, but she *did* care about Dave. Katie was always advising her to share a boy's interests, and maybe she should give it a try. If it made Dave like her better, it was worth it.

"It was great," she said with a bright smile, amazed at how easy it was to lie. "I'm so glad we came," she added, this time meaning the words.

David smiled down at her. She had obviously given him the right answer. "I'm glad we came, too," he said, helping her on with her jacket.

Sara felt warm all over. She was very pleased with herself. For once she hadn't bungled everything.

Chuck and Anita caught up with them in the lobby. "How about going out for some pizza?" he suggested.

Dave glanced at Sara for a second, then shook his head. "Maybe next time," he said. "I'll see you tomorrow."

Sara was surprised that Dave would turn Chuck down. It could only mean that he was anxious to get her home. She had thought the evening was going well, but maybe she was wrong.

When they stepped out into the cool October night air, Dave put his arm around her waist. "I love the fall. This kind of weather makes me feel alive," he said, inhaling deeply.

"Me, too," Sara agreed enthusiastically. She wasn't fibbing that time. Fall made her think of juicy McIntosh apples and roaring fires in fireplaces. It rivaled spring as her favorite season.

"I know a place where they serve a mean hot chocolate," suggested Dave, opening the car door for her.

"I'd love one."

"Then we're off," he said, climbing in beside her and starting the engine.

Sara was surprised to see that they were heading toward the shore. The houses in that part of town were all large and expensive, surrounded by beautifully manicured lawns and well-tended gardens.

"I didn't know there were any restaurants open down here at this time of year," she said.

"There aren't." Dave smiled slyly.

"What do you mean?" Sara was puzzled.

"This is my stomping ground," he explained. "I live down here, and I know all the ins and outs of the area," he said mysteriously.

Sara hadn't realized that Dave's family lived by the water, but it did make sense. She knew he was well-off. Come to think of it, Julie Redman lived somewhere around there, too. It was probably where most of the "in" crowd lived, Sara thought. Money is one of the criteria for belonging to their group.

Dave pulled into a tiny parking lot beside a small building with a bright green- and white-striped awning. The sign on the front door read "Angelina's Bakery."

"But bakeries don't serve hot chocolate," Sara protested.

"This one does," said David. "The best—with chocolate imported from Italy," he added.

As he pushed open the glass door, a bell tinkled overhead. A pretty young woman who looked about their age or a little older stepped out from behind the counter. Her long black hair was tied in a thick braid that fell halfway down her back, and her dark eyes were full of smiles when she saw Dave.

She gave him a warm hug, then stepped back to get a good look at him.

"Maria, when did you get back from Italy?" he asked.

"Only last week. Mama said that she hadn't seen you in a while, and I was hoping that you would stop in," she said.

"If I had known you were back, I would have been in sooner," he said sincerely.

The girl turned her attention to Sara. "Watch out for this one," she advised with a smile, waving her finger in a playful warning.

Sara smiled back. It was impossible not to. The girl was full of warmth and energy, and her relationship with Dave seemed more sisterly than romantic.

"What can I get for you and your friend?"

"Two of your delicious hot chocolates," said David. "With extra whipped cream."

31

"And two cannoli?" Maria asked over her shoulder as she hurried off to get their order.

"Well, now that you mention it, I could manage one." David laughed. He led Sara to a small, white wrought iron table in the corner.

"I never even knew this place existed," said Sara. "And I've lived in Stanford all my life."

"Most of the people who came to Angelina's live nearby," said David. "It's such a small place that outsiders don't know it exists. But once they find it, they come back again and again." He reached for Sara's hand across the table.

Maria was soon placing two steaming mugs of hot chocolate and a plate of flaky pastry rolls stuffed to the edges with thick, creamy filling on the table. She lingered for a moment.

"Have you done much fishing lately?" she asked Dave, a smile of interest lighting her eyes.

"Not too much during the summer. Dad was having some trouble with the boat. But we just got back from a weekend up in Quincy, and we caught a whole slew of flounder. Do you want to come along the next time we go to Massachusetts?" he asked with a teasing smile.

"No, thank you. You always make me bait my own hook, and I can't stand to spear those worms." She wrinkled her nose in distaste. "Do you like to fish?" She turned her attention to Sara.

"I really don't know. I've never tried," said Sara. She didn't think it was something she'd find enjoyable, especially from Maria's description of baiting hooks. But if it was something Dave liked doing, then she'd take a neutral position.

"I'll take you out sometime," Dave promised. "And I've got a feeling you'll be a great fisherman."

Sara smiled at the compliment. Dave was really being too wonderful to her. She wished their date never had to end. "How long have you two known each other?" she asked Maria, curious about his relationship with the other girl.

"Forever!" Maria laughed. "My mama used to cook for David's family. She and Mrs. Reiner became very good friends, and David's mother helped us to start this shop." Maria waved her graceful arms around the bakery.

Sara was surprised at Maria's honesty. Not too many people she knew would have admitted that their mother had been a cook for somebody else's family. But Maria wasn't ashamed of it, and Sara admired her and liked her for that. She was certainly different from the other girls in Dave's crowd—she was *real*. Sara found herself wondering if they might ever have dated each other.

"Isn't this the best hot chocolate you've ever tasted?" asked Dave, finishing his to the last drop.

"It really is—and the best pastry," Sara agreed.

"Nobody makes better Italian pastries than Angelina," said Dave. "But we'd better get going before I polish off another one of those cannoli, Maria. I promised Sara's mother I wouldn't get her home too late."

"Then you'd better hustle. You don't want her to think you're a naughty boy," she said with a teasing smile as she collected the empty cups from the table. "It was very nice meeting you, Sara. I hope we'll see each other again."

"So do I." Sara waved as she followed Dave to the door.

This time Dave put on a romantic Lionel Ritchie tape, and Sara leaned her head back against the seat and closed her eyes. If she let her imagination go, she could almost believe that the Camaro was a magical ship, and that she was floating through the night.

She felt so safe with him. It had been a

wonderful evening. She only hoped it had been as special for him.

She got her answer when he pulled into her driveway and parked, then turned in his seat so that he was facing her. "I don't know why it took me so long to ask you out," he said, his voice hushed and low in the darkness. "But I promise that it won't be this long again." He tilted his head and brought his lips down on hers.

Sara stiffened in his arms. She wanted Dave to kiss her—she wanted it more than anything—but suddenly it was all going much too fast. This was only their first date, and Dave was acting as if they'd been going out for months.

He kissed her gently and then drew back. "I won't rush you," he said as if reading her mind.

Sara swallowed hard. *Why don't I know what to do and how to act?* she thought desperately.

Dave came around to her side of the car and walked her to the front door.

"How about helping out a suffering fellow student on Monday?" he suggested, putting a hand firmly and affectionately on her shoulder. "I have a big Spanish test on Tuesday, and I'd really appreciate any help that you could give me," he added earnestly.

Sara was flattered that he would ask for her help, and relieved that he wasn't annoyed at her for rejecting him in the car.

"I'd love to," she said sincerely. "I can meet you in the library after school."

"It's a date," agreed Dave, planting a quick kiss on her forehead. Then, before she realized what had happened, he was back in his car and pulling out of the driveway.

Sara stood at her front door for several minutes before she went in, gazing up at the yellow October moon crisscrossed by bare branches, her blue eyes dreamy. It had been an evening she'd never forget.

Chapter Three

"I am absolutely dying to hear all about it," declared Katie. She was standing behind Sara in the hot-lunch line in the school cafeteria.

"This is the most wonderful Monday of my life." Sara sighed. "All I can say is that Saturday night was so spectacular that even this"— she waved an unappetizing hot dog at her friend—"can't get me down!" Katie giggled. Sara pushed her tray along the rack and added a container of milk and a brownie to her meal.

"Then it *must* have been incredible." Katie shook her head in astonishment.

Sara nodded. "I think I'm in love," she whispered as she dug into her wallet to pay for her lunch.

"Uh-oh." Katie rolled her blue eyes. "Don't say that." The two girls sat down at an empty table.

"Why not?" asked Sara defensively. "Dave is beyond a shadow of a doubt the most wonderful boy in the whole world."

"Do you know the crowd he runs around with?" Katie bit into her hot dog and then made a wry face as a blob of mustard squirted out onto the sleeve of her turquoise sweater dress. "Shoot!"

"Do you mean guys like Chuck Taylor?" asked Sara, anxious to show Katie how wrong she was about Dave.

Katie nodded, her mouth too full of another bite of hot dog to talk.

"I met him and Anita Marcus at the movies on Saturday night, and they seemed nice enough." Sara opened her milk carton waiting for Katie's reaction. She didn't have to wait long.

"Anita Marcus?" squealed Katie. She lowered her voice. "Are you kidding? She's one of the most stuck-up snobs at Stanford. Not to mention the fact that she also happens to be Julie Redman's best friend."

"I'm not going to hold Dave's friends against him," Sara said firmly. She only wished it was as easily said as done. "Besides Chuck and Anita haven't done anything to us, we don't have any right to judge them."

"Sara, when you go out with a guy, you hang around with his crowd. Do you really think you'll feel comfortable paling around with Anita Marcus?" Katie asked earnestly.

"I don't know, Katie. Anita and I will never be best friends the way you and I are, but I can't let that get in the way of my relationship with Dave."

"I'm sorry." Katie apologized when she saw the worry in Sara's eyes. "I didn't mean to upset you. It's just that I'm not so sure Dave Reiner is the right boy for you." She patted Sara's arm and then reached for her apple.

Sara felt herself growing angry. "I don't understand you, Katie." The apple stopped midway to Katie's mouth. "You never stop nagging me to go on dates, you're constantly trying to fix me up with every friend or relative Jason's ever had, but now when I've finally found a guy on my own to go out with you decide he's not perfect enough for me." Sara's heart was hammering, and her cheeks were fiery red.

"It's just because I care about you," insisted Katie, becoming upset herself. "I think we're attracting a crowd," she whispered, nodding toward a table across the cafeteria.

Sara followed her friend's glance, and found

herself staring into a pair of hostile emerald green eyes. Julie Redman and Anita Marcus were deep in conversation, pausing just at that moment to stare in Sara's direction.

Looking at the other girls and having them look at her made Sara suddenly feel that she was crazy ever to have thought that a guy like Dave could really like her.

"Don't bother saying it." Sara sighed, putting up her hands in surrender. "I can't bear to hear 'I told you so,' " she said dismally.

"I wasn't going to say that," Katie said loyally. "I *am* on your side. Remember?"

"You guys look like your best friend just died, but here I am alive and kicking!" Marsha set her stack of books down on the table with a thud.

Sara couldn't help smiling at her friend's banter. "Where have you been? Lunch is almost over!"

"Actually, there's something I'd like to talk to you about," said Marsha. "Do you know my friend Rick Davenport? He's a copy editor for the paper."

Sara and Katie nodded. Marsha paused, running her fingers briskly through her short, tousled hair.

"Well, Rick gave me a copy of an article that's going to be in the next issue of the

Star," she explained with a funny look at Sara.

"Well, what's it about? Let me guess—your affair with the captain of the chess team has been exposed," said Katie, trying to tease Marsha out of her serious mood.

"I wish," said Marsha, thrusting the photocopied paper under her friend's nose.

Katie scanned the page. "Uh-oh," she said, shaking her head and handing the paper on to Sara.

Sara took it. "What's the problem?" she asked. Then she saw the familiar byline: David Reiner.

The article, entitled "May The Spirits Be With You," was all about the upcoming Halloween dance. "All the credit for this ghoulishly delightful transformation of our school goes to one talented junior, Sara Grant." Sara looked up in embarrassment at her friends.

"I honestly don't know where he got such a ridiculous idea," she insisted helplessly. She felt terrible. She knew how hard her friends had worked on the decorations; it was wrong that she should be given all the credit.

"Maybe Dave's a little prejudiced," Marsha said quietly, avoiding Sara's eyes. Sara stiffened, and her eyes flashed with anger.

"Come on, Marsha. This isn't Sara's fault,"

interrupted Katie. "I don't think she had anything to do with this article. You know better than that."

Marsha looked from Sara to Katie, and then back to Sara again. "I'm sorry, Sara. I didn't mean to blame you for what Dave wrote," she said sincerely. "It's just that I spent a lot of time on those decorations, too, and it's so unfair that Dave never bothers to mention Katie or me even once."

Sara softened. "I can't believe he didn't mention your names, either. But maybe I can get him to change it. After all, it hasn't been printed yet," she said hopefully, wanting to make everything up to her friends.

"No, that's OK. All our friends know that the three of us worked on this project together, and that's all that counts. Just forget about it, Sara." Katie jumped into her usual role as peacemaker.

"But that's not fair," Sara insisted. She *had* told Dave that she didn't do the decorating on her own, but he just hadn't listened to her. No matter what Katie said, she'd have to speak to him about it and make sure the article was rewritten.

"Well, if it isn't the Three Musketeers," said a deep male voice.

All three heads turned at the same time,

just as Jason Prescott straddled the bench seat with one long leg and sat down opposite Katie.

He put his finger under her chin. "Hey, funny face, what's the matter? You all look like you just got kicked out of school."

"It's nothing, Jason." Katie smiled and leaned across the table to brush Jason's lips with her own.

They made a terrific couple. They had a lot in common—they both loved acting, and together they were a major force in the Drama Club. They even looked a little alike, Sara thought, with the same bright blond hair and deep blue eyes.

"You could have fooled me." Jason still looked concerned.

"Just girl stuff!" Katie waved aside his worried frown. "Come on, hit us with your latest one-liners. I live for them," she said, taking his hands in her own.

Jason smiled brightly. "If you insist," he said.

Even Sara had to smile, forgetting for a minute about Dave's article. Jason was an incurable joke-teller. Unfortunately, however, he got most of his material from his eight-year-old brother, Bobby, which was a good indication of the level of the humor.

"OK, are you sure you're ready for this? Bobby says it's the hit of the third grade," warned Jason, setting the stage for his performance.

"Come on, you ham." Katie laughed, punching him lightly on the arm.

"This girl never gets enough of me, like the rest of my adoring public." He winked at Sara and Marsha.

"Jason Prescott, if you don't tell us your dumb joke in the next two seconds, I'll upstage you at the next Drama Club rehearsal!"

"Anything but that!" Jason relented with a grin. "What did the grape say when the elephant stepped on it?"

The three girls exchanged glances. "I have absolutely no idea," Katie conceded finally.

Jason smiled broadly. "It didn't say a word. It just let out a little wine."

The girls groaned, as Jason protested, "Come on, that one was pretty good, admit it."

"Hit us with your second shot." Katie put up her fists and stuck out her chin.

"Oh, you're asking for it today. Now for the second-prize winner in Mrs. Gillespie's third grade," he announced, "How do you keep a rhinoceros from charging?" He paused for just a second. "Give up?" he asked hopefully.

"OK, but only because you're dying to tell us," said Katie.

"You take away his credit card." Jason spread his hands wide as if the answer should have been obvious.

"Ouch!" cried Katie.

Sara and Marsha were laughing, too. "If only I had a younger brother or sister," said Katie, "then I could beat your jokes for sure. But I don't have any secret sources."

"That's a classic excuse." Jason shrugged triumphantly. "Bobby scours his school for jokes every day, and I only have to pay him a quarter apiece. You could never top that," Jason said as he stood up and walked around the table to where Katie sat. "Come on, Lazybones," he said, pulling her to her feet.

"We'll see you guys later," said Katie, her arm around Jason's waist.

"See you, Katie." Marsha saluted her friend with a tuna fish sandwich.

"I'll call you tonight," promised Sara, knowing she wouldn't have a chance to see her after school. She'd promised David she'd tutor him that day, and besides, she was anxious to talk to him about his article.

As the last period of the day drew to a close, Sara was filled with a mixture of anxiety and anticipation. She was nervous about seeing Dave again; what if Saturday night had been just another date for him? He might just treat her casually, as if nothing had happened between them. Either way, the prospect of being with him made her heart race. She couldn't help hoping for the best.

She spent a long time at her locker, deliberately dragging out the process of deciding which books she'd need for her homework that night. Then, glancing at her watch, she realized she'd better quit stalling or Dave might think she wasn't going to show up at all.

She slammed her locker door shut with a bang and ran down the long hallway, her low-heeled shoes clattering on the tile floor and her brown canvas bag swinging over her shoulder. When she got to the library she didn't see Dave at first. She wandered over to the first section of study tables and spotted him leaning back in his chair, one leg crossed over the other knee and one foot on the ground for balance. He was deeply engrossed in a magazine and hadn't noticed Sara come in.

She walked up behind him and glanced over his shoulder. "Studying?" she asked with a teasing smile.

Dave jumped and his chair hit the ground

with a bang. The magazine slapped shut. "You caught me!" He grinned and held up a copy of *Fisherman's World*.

"That's OK, you were on free time," said Sara. She wanted to say something about the article he had written for the school paper, but she wasn't quite sure how to begin. He might think she was criticizing him, and anyway, she wasn't even supposed to have seen it yet.

"Well, I'm ready whenever you are," said Dave, breaking into her thoughts. He slid his chair in closer to the table and opened his Spanish book.

"Sure, I'm ready, too." Sara decided it would be better to wait awhile before she said anything. "What's your test on tomorrow?" she asked.

"Idiomatic expressions. Good old Senora Killjoy, I mean Killroy"—he looked at Sara for a response to his pun and she smiled faintly—"loves idiomatic expressions. That's all she's talked about for the past two weeks. And tomorrow, as she so eloquently put it, she'll pick our brains for the fruits of her labor." Dave made a disgusted face as he mimicked the teachers.

Sara felt pulled in two directions. She knew Dave wanted her to agree with him that Senora Killroy was a tyrant, but the truth was that Sara really liked her. Once again, however, she decided the safest bet was to say nothing at all. "Well, there are lots of different idioms, Dave. In this chapter they're talking about weather expressions, like ¿*Que tiempo hace?* which means 'How is the weather?' "

Sara felt a little awkward playing tutor to Dave. She wished she could feel as comfortable with him as Katie did with Jason. For some reason, she just didn't feel like she could relax completely and be herself when she was with him. But that wasn't really fair. Katie had known Jason forever, and she and Dave had just started to get to know each other.

She looked up to find Dave staring at her.

"You're a genius, did you know that?" he said with a charming smile.

Sara felt her cheeks burning. She was embarrassed—Dave would have to be blind not to see the effect he had on her.

"I don't think knowing a few Spanish idioms really puts me in the genius category," she said, brushing aside the compliment. "Idioms are just certain ways of saying things, and they need to be memorized, that's all."

"It's a lot more than that," said Dave. "I'll bet you're a top student in all your subjects."

Sara was worried that he might think she was some kind of bookworm. He wasn't exactly the type to date a girl with that reputation. "Not in all my subjects," she hastened to assure him, even though she was a good all-around student. There *were* a couple of classes she had to try harder in than others, like math.

"What do *you* think of old Killjoy?" Dave abandoned idioms for a moment.

Sara was on the spot. "I don't know, I guess she's OK," she said, feeling guilty and uncomfortable.

"Oh, come on Sara, nobody really likes that old windbag. She gets a kick out of failing students. As a matter of fact, she looks a lot like one of those witches you've got hanging up in the hallways." He laughed and reached for Sara's hand.

Sara's smile was insincere, and she felt like a traitor. But she was under David's spell. Whenever he touched her or looked in her eyes she forgot about everything except how he made her feel, and that was wonderful.

"Now you're the kind of teacher I'd like to have," said David softly as he ran his thumb slowly over her knuckles.

Sara felt herself getting that breathless, floating sensation again. "We'd better get back to those idioms." She forced herself to focus on the open textbook.

Dave smiled his sexy, lopsided smile. "OK, teach, let's hit those books," he agreed, keeping hold of her hand and moving his chair slightly closer to hers.

It took all of Sara's willpower to concentrate on the Spanish grammar, but she was determined to help David pass his exam. Maybe if they were successful at working together that time, he'd call her about his next test. It might not be a date, but it was better than nothing.

"*Hace bien tiempo* means 'the weather is fine.'" But only part of Sara's mind was on idiomatic expressions. A very small part. Most of her was tingling as Dave squeezed her hand and sent butterflies dancing around her heart.

Chapter Four

Sara watched as Abby's velvety gray-brown ears stood straight up at attention. The dog cocked her head to one side, listening intently, and then hoisted herself up on all four legs and belly-flopped off the bed.

"Oh, Abby, look what you've done!" Sara lunged for the papers and books that went flying in every direction. She landed flat on her stomach with her head hanging over the side of the bed and her hair trailing on the carpet just as her mother walked in.

So that's why you gave up your comfy position, you bad dog, Sara thought. *You know very well you're not allowed on the furniture. You heard Mom coming!*

"What on earth are you doing?" Mrs. Grant shook her head at the disarray.

"Oh, hi, Mom. I was just getting some notes together for Dave," explained Sara, returning to an upright position. "He's been having a little trouble with Spanish, and I promised to help him bring up his grade."

"Didn't you just tutor him the other day?" Mrs. Grant stopped to pick up a wayward paper.

Sara nodded. "Yeah, but we only went over a little grammar. There's a lot more we still have to cover," she said, gathering the papers and piling them into a neat stack in front of her.

"Then you'll be seeing Dave again?"

"Oh, sure," said Sara. "I'm meeting him in the library tomorrow afternoon." The next day was Thursday, three long days since she had last studied with him. She could hardly wait to see him again—she knew she had better start thinking about what to wear!

"I mean on a date. Do you think you'll be going out with him some time soon?" asked Mrs. Grant.

Sara pushed the curls back from her forehead and looked dreamily at her mother. "I don't know, Mom. I really hope so, though. Don't you think he's gorgeous?"

Mrs. Grant smiled. "He *is* handsome, honey, but you know there's a lot more to a relationship than that."

"Of course I do, Mom, but Dave and I get along really well," said Sara. "You told me how important it is for a couple to have things in common, and I think I'm finally beginning to understand what you mean."

"I hope so, dear. A relationship where two people really share the same interests has a much greater chance of lasting."

Sara considered her mother seriously. Mrs. Grant's hair was as curly as Sara's, but it was cut quite short and threaded with silver. Mother and daughter had the same blue eyes and gentle smiles. It really meant a lot to Sara that her mother should know she wasn't a baby anymore, that she was capable of having a mature relationship. She'd approve of the way Sara was handling things with Dave. Wouldn't she?

It was obvious to Sara that it pleased Dave when she pretended to like the movie they saw together, even though she hadn't really liked it at all. And she was determined to learn all that she could about fishing. She had bought a copy of *Fisherman's World* and was going to read it as soon as she had a free minute. She'd prove to Dave they were perfect for each other.

"Don't worry, Mom. I've found the most fantastic boy in the whole world, and everything is going to work out great," said Sara with a confident smile.

"I'm afraid Dave and Abby didn't get off to a very good start, though," her mother said with a laugh as the dog nuzzled her hand, begging to be petted.

"I know." Sara's smile faded momentarily. It kind of bothered her that Dave didn't seem to be very fond of animals. But who could blame him for not being wild about being slobbered over and trampled on by a Great Dane?

Sara loved animals, dogs in particular. She planned to own a huge kennel one day—it would be the most modern facility in the whole state of Connecticut, and people would come from all over the state to get Sara's special care for their pets.

"Dave's just not used to having dogs around," said Sara, anxious to excuse Dave's behavior. "He told me he'd never had a dog. His mother thinks they make too much of a mess in the house."

Mrs. Grant raised her eyebrows. "That's too

54

bad," she said. "But maybe he and Abby will become friends."

"I don't doubt it, if Abby has any say in the matter." Sara grinned. "Her goal in life is to give and receive affection. Who can resist her?"

"I'm sure everything will work out fine, honey." Mrs. Grant bent down to brush Sara's forehead with her lips. "Don't stay up too late."

"I won't, Mom." Sara opened the Spanish textbook and propped it on her knees as her mother closed the bedroom door behind her.

Abby stared at the door cautiously for a full minute. Then she leaped back on the bed and resettled herself at Sara's feet.

"Good timing, girl." Sara giggled. Soon she was intently making a list of vocabulary words to go over with David. *El sillon*, armchair. *La cortina*, curtain. She'd be so proud if he raised his grade for the next report card. And he would—with her help, of course.

She worked for another half hour until her eyelids grew heavy and the Spanish words for sugar and pepper started to run together. She put the books aside and leaned back against her pillows, the copy of *Fisherman's World* in her hand. If she could keep her eyes open for another few minutes she could begin that article about freshwater fishing and after that possibly learn some of the finer points of shrimp trawling. But it was no use. The magazine fell from her hand to the carpet where it lay until the next morning when she carefully propped it on her desk to remind herself to read it. She just had to learn to love what Dave loved, and then maybe—just maybe—he'd learn to love her.

"You did all this for me?" Dave stared with amazement at the handwritten list of vocabulary words Sara handed him.

"Sure! I thought if you could see them all out in front of you like this, it would be easier for you to memorize them," she explained.

"I can't believe you went to all this trouble. You're incredible, you know that?" he said, cupping her chin in his hand.

His blue eyes drank in hers, and Sara's heart sped up to its by-now-familiar Kentucky Derby pace. Her breath came in unsteady little puffs. She was sure Dave was going to kiss her, and she closed her eyes in anticipation.

"This *is* a school library, to be used for studying, not dating."

Sara's eyes flew open, and she jumped at the sound of the dry, raspy voice. She found herself staring into the grave, lined face of the head librarian, Mrs. O'Neill. Nobody in the school was quite sure how old Mrs. O'Neill really was, but most people figured she had reached retirement age long ago—she just couldn't bring herself to leave.

"Sorry, Miss O'Neill, I guess we just got carried away," said David, flashing his irresistible smile.

The librarian's expression softened slightly, and Sara thought she almost saw her smile before she turned on her heel and marched back to her desk. Sara was stunned. There didn't seem to be *anybody* Dave couldn't charm.

"How'd you do that?" Sara gasped, staring at the librarian's retreating back. "She would have given anyone else a detention."

Dave grinned. "She's really just an old pussycat."

"I never thought of her quite like that," whispered Sara with a giggle.

"Don't worry about her," said Dave. "We've got more important things to talk about. Like the show at the armory in Cheshire on Sunday. All the newest kinds of fishing equipment will be on display. How about going with me?"

Sara didn't know what to say. This was what she had been waiting for, another date with Dave. But to a fishing equipment exhibition? She'd been hoping for something a little more romantic.

Dave was looking at her expectantly, waiting for an answer. "Is there some problem with Sunday?" he asked. "Do you already have plans?"

Sara was startled out of her thoughts. "No, I don't have any other plans," she admitted quickly. "I'd love to go to the show with you." So what if it wasn't something she'd necessarily enjoy doing herself. She'd be Dave's date, and that was all that mattered.

"Hey, that's terrific. Why don't we call it quits on studying for today? I've got to go to the Student Activities Council meeting." He closed his Spanish book and pushed his chair away from the table.

"Are you a member?"

"No, but I have to cover their meetings for the *Star*," he said with a grimace.

Sara had always wanted to be on the Student Activities Council, but she was too shy to run for any election. "It must be really interesting to hear firsthand about all the activities that'll be going on at school. I remember that article you wrote about the football rally. It was great," she said enthusiastically. *I remember every article you ever wrote,* she added silently. *Including the one about the Halloween dance,* a guilty voice inside of her added. But Sara kept quiet, not wanting to say anything that might make Dave mad.

Dave nodded. "Yeah, that was one of my better pieces, but that's because I liked the subject. Some of the ideas the council comes up with are pretty dull," he said.

"Then why don't you get someone else to cover the meetings?" she suggested.

"As if I haven't tried!" He shrugged. "But everybody on the paper is overworked, so I'm stuck with it. This guy, Chris Forrester, is head of the committee, and he insists that the meetings should be covered. He thinks the *Star's* got some kind of obligation to keep students informed of every move they make." Dave rolled his eyes toward the ceiling.

Sara thought Chris had a good point but she didn't say that to Dave. Things were going so well between them that she didn't want to rock the boat in any way.

"I still envy you," insisted Sara. "It was the Student Activities Council that came up with the idea for the Halloween Costume Dance. All the kids seem to love *that* idea."

"Well I didn't say they were nerds all the time. The Halloween Dance is a great idea, except for one little thing."

Sara looked at him questioningly.

"You haven't agreed to go with me yet," Dave said quietly.

Sara's heart stopped dead in her chest and then started up again at twice its normal speed. For a second she felt as she had the day she'd gotten her wisdom teeth pulled and had had laughing gas—definitely light-headed. This was her dream come true! Not only was she being asked to the Halloween Dance, but by Dave Reiner, one of the most popular and best-looking boys at Stanford High. He really liked her!

"What does that dead silence mean? Yes or no?" David smiled confidently as he reached for Sara's hand.

"Yes, oh definitely yes," she said breathily. She was so excited, she had to force herself not to run around the library yelling at the top of her lungs that Dave Reiner had invited her to the dance.

"Bingo, you gave the right answer." Dave squeezed her hand tightly in his own. "Now all we've got to decide is how we're going to dress so that we'll win first prize for best costumes."

Sara's mind raced. She wanted to come up with a dynamite idea right on the spot.

But Dave was talking to himself. "Let me think about it for a while," he mused. "Maybe

I'll have a brainstorm by Sunday. I'd give you a ride home, but as I said, I'm stuck here with the meeting." He paused at the door to the library.

"Oh, that's OK," Sara assured him. "Dave, do you think I could sit in on one of those meetings sometime?" she asked timidly.

"Hey, that's a great idea!" His eyes brightened. "You could even go without me, kind of like my stand-in. If I was busy doing something else, you could go instead, pinch hit for me." He nodded enthusiastically.

Sara's eyes gave away her confusion, but Dave didn't seem to notice. That really wasn't what she had had in mind at all. She didn't want to go to the meetings without Dave—the point was to spend as much time with him as possible, doing something they both liked.

Everything they did, like the fishing equipment show, seemed to be for Dave with her included as an afterthought. Not that Sara really minded. She guessed the important thing was that he wanted her company. Maybe it was too much to ask that he should want her input as well.

And if it would help him out for her to take his place at one or two of the meetings, then what could be the harm?

"Sure, I could do that," she agreed with a warm smile.

"You've got a deal, Sara Grant," he said, stooping to kiss her quickly. "I'm off. See you Sunday, if not before," he called over his shoulder as he hurried down the hall, his white sneakers hitting the tile with force and energy.

Sara watched until he was out of sight, and then she continued on out of the building. The days were starting to get chilly, she thought as she hugged her sweater tightly around her.

"Need a ride, babe?"

Sara turned as a blue Honda pulled to a stop in front of her.

"I heard your car was in the shop, so I'm gallantly offering to give you a lift home." Katie stuck her head out of the car window.

"Just in time to save me from a walk home!" Sara climbed gratefully into the passenger seat.

"I know what you mean." Katie giggled, peering over her shoulder as she pulled out of the parking lot and onto the busy road.

"Katie, I have the most fantastic news." Sara grabbed her friend's arm, causing the car to veer crazily for a second. "Oops, sorry!"

Katie shook her head. "It must be love.

What else could make such a sane and responsible person like you act so crazy?"

"It is. It really is," agreed Sara, bubbling with enthusiasm. She felt so happy, she thought she might burst. "Dave asked me to the Halloween dance. Now I'll be going just like you and Marsha!"

"Sara, that *is* great!" Katie exclaimed sincerely. "I felt guilty about going to the dance without you. I even felt bad talking about it in front of you, and there we all were working on the decorations together."

Katie's remark raised a sore subject, one that Sara didn't want to think about. She was annoyed at herself for not mentioning the newspaper article to Dave. He definitely should have included Katie and Marsha's names in the piece, but she hadn't said anything about it. Maybe he thought he was doing something nice for her by giving her all the credit for the decorations. Maybe it was his way of letting everybody know he liked her. Sara felt warm at the thought. The last thing she'd want would be for him to think she was ungrateful and critical of what he'd written.

"Now we can all hang out at the dance together," said Katie with a happy smile. "I don't think Jason and Dave really know each other, but this will be a great chance for them to get acquainted."

Sara nodded, but she couldn't manage much of a smile. Dave would probably want to hang out with his own friends at the dance, and she didn't know what that would mean for her.

"What's the matter? You don't look very happy all of a sudden," observed Katie.

"It's nothing." Sara looked out the window to avoid her friend's penetrating gaze. She'd just have to handle the situation if and when it arose. Besides, she was sure Dave would be reasonable—he'd understand that it was important for her to spend time with her friends, too.

"I was just wondering what Dave and I might dress up as," Sara said lamely.

"Oh, you'll get one of your brainstorms." Katie waved a hand sparkling with brightly polished nails. "Did I tell you Jason and I decided to go as a sixties couple? You know, bell-bottom hip-huggers and white lipstick. I'm going to have fun putting everything together. I was thinking of checking out that costume rental store downtown. Even if you don't rent anything, you can get some terrific ideas. Do you want to come along?"

"That's a great idea," Sara said. "How about

Saturday afternoon?" She wanted to go before her date with Dave on Sunday so she could surprise him by having their costumes all worked out.

"Sure. Maybe we can work in some real everyday clothes shopping, too." Katie smiled slyly. "I've got thirty dollars saved up, and it's burning a hole in my pocket."

Sara laughed. She felt carefree and happy. She was the luckiest girl in the world! The sun was shining, she had great friends, and she was falling in love with a wonderful boy. Best of all, he was falling in love with her, too! Things had never been better.

Chapter Five

"Saturday afternoon at the mall is like vacationing in a sardine can," Katie said with a sigh.

Sara laughed as she watched Katie adjust her neon-pink headband. "I can't remember crowds ever stopping you before. You're the most dedicated shopper I know."

Katie shrugged, her face brightening as she spotted a colorful display of sweaters. "Oh, Sara, let's stop here for a second, OK?"

"I should have known we'd never get more than two feet into this place without you finding something to buy!"

"But isn't this the most gorgeous sweater you've ever seen?" Katie held up a lime green knit top with a low *V* neckline. "This would look great with my new harem pants," she mused, peeking at the price tag.

Sara watched Katie quickly put the sweater down, as though it had turned into a hot potato in her hands. "How much is it?"

"Would you believe sixty bucks?" Katie shook her blond head. "It's enough to make me take up knitting again."

"Forget about it," exclaimed Sara. "Don't you remember that scarf you knitted in the fifth grade? You dropped so many stitches it ended up looking like a piece of Swiss cheese."

Katie laughed. "You're right, I remember that. I guess I'd just better earn some more money baby-sitting. Everything that catches my eye is always so expensive." She steered her friend toward a cookie stand. "Just look at those gooey, chocolaty cookies, Sara. Help me resist the temptation."

"Are you kidding? I don't have any more willpower than you do!" Sara's mouth was watering at the delicious aroma.

"Then we'd better get out of here fast. Let's hurry over to the costume shop. Now don't look to your right or left," warned Katie, taking Sara's hand and pulling her along.

"I hope Dave's not going to want to be something too flashy for Halloween," said Sara as they entered the glass elevator that would take them up to the fifth floor. "That's not really my style."

"I'd say you've done a pretty good job of handling him so far. You seem to know exactly what he likes," said Katie.

Sara glanced at her friend. She wasn't quite sure what to make of Katie's tone.

"Don't you like Dave, Katie?" she asked, concerned. Katie was her oldest and dearest friend, but she cared about Dave now, too. She didn't want to be caught between the two.

Katie met Sara's eyes for a long moment, and then she looked away. "Sure I do," she said as the elevator stopped and the doors slid open. "And I'm sure David will love whatever costume you choose. Come on, there's The Costume Wizard!" The girls approached the glittering store.

"Well, I wish I could be so sure." Sara studied the weirdly dressed mannequins in the window, a dubious expression on her face.

"What do you think about this?" Katie pointed to a suede-fringed dress. "You could go as a cowgirl, and Dave could be a Wild West sheriff."

Sara shook her head. "Definitely not. That's too old-fashioned, not funky enough. And besides, Dave isn't exactly the cowboy type. Can you picture him riding his trusty old horse across the prairie?"

"You're right. Then what about something from *Star Wars*?" Katie posed next to a mannequin dressed as Chewbacca.

Sara giggled. "Dave is already cuddly. He doesn't need a hairy old costume. And *Star Wars* is out now, way out."

"Right again." Katie threw her hands up in the air. "Well, I'll make one last suggestion. How about going as a mermaid? Mermaids never go out of style."

"Oh, Katie, I'm just going to have to do this on my own. I mean, I know you have good intentions, but seriously! That mermaid thing is cut so low in front that my parents would never let me out of the house in it."

Katie glanced wistfully at the tight-fitting, iridescent costume. "Well, don't say that I didn't try," she said pointedly.

Katie sank into a chair near one of the dressing rooms, and Sara set off to wander around the crowded store by herself. She considered his-and-her clown costumes—bright baggy pants and red suspenders—but decided against them. She was looking for something really special. She wanted to surprise Dave, make him proud of her creativity.

Suddenly Sara's eyes were caught by the prettiest pair of gold hoop earrings she had ever seen. Perfectly round, in a delicate and unusual braid design, they gleamed as brightly as diamonds.

Sara couldn't see the face of the girl wearing them because she was kneeling in front of a little boy, helping him position a pirate's patch on one eye. She stepped slightly closer and stared at the thick braid of shiny dark hair that lay against the girl's back. Something about the girl was familiar.

"Dominick, you look like a real pirate now, I promise you," the girl said as she stood up and handed the child a long plastic sword.

"Are you sure, Maria? Are you positively, absolutely sure?" he demanded.

Just as the girl turned, Sara remembered. They saw each other at the same moment and smiled.

"You're Maria, from Angelina's, aren't you?" asked Sara, surprised by how happy she was to see the other girl.

Maria nodded. "And you're Sara, Dave's friend. It's so good to see you again," she said with a warm and sincere smile. "Are you shopping for a costume for a little brother or sister?" Maria nodded at Dominick who was now fencing with an invisible opponent.

Sara shook her head, she felt a little embarrassed to admit that she was looking for one for herself. "Not really. Dave and I are going to a Halloween dance at our school, and I was trying to get some ideas. Your earrings just inspired me, though. They're really beautiful."

Maria smiled. "Thank you. They were a gift, from my grandparents in Italy," she said, reaching up to touch the gold hoops. "Don't keep me in suspense, Sara. What are you going to be?"

"Something I've always dreamed of being, a real fantasy of mine," admitted Sara. "I'd love to dress up as a gypsy in a wild, exotic costume." She shrugged to cover up her shyness. It wasn't like her to confide such a thing to someone she hardly knew. "I don't know, something colorful and romantic."

"That's a great idea," said Maria, clapping her hands together.

"But do you think Dave will like the idea?"

"What does it matter? He doesn't have to go dressed as a gypsy," she said. "He can be whatever he likes."

Sara nodded. "I know, but he *is* my date, and I don't want him to—well, you know—" she hedged, not wanting to admit how insecure she was in her relationship with Dave.

"Sara, let me tell you something. Learn to please yourself. You'll never win if you're always going to try and please Dave." Maria's tone was sympathetic but firm. "Nobody can always satisfy someone else's wishes."

Sara didn't know what to say. She couldn't exactly tell Maria that that was a pretty easy philosophy to live by if you weren't trying to keep Dave Reiner as a boyfriend. But she was, and she planned to be successful.

At that moment the little boy came running up to Maria and threw his arms around her waist. "Can I really keep all of this stuff, Maria?" he squealed excitedly.

Maria smiled at him. "You bet, Dommy." She turned back to Sara. "This is my brother, Dominick. Dominick, Sara's a gypsy princess. What do you think about that?"

"Are you really?" he asked, impressed.

"Well, not quite, but I'll be one on Halloween at least."

"Cute kid," said Katie, joining the group.

Sara introduced the two girls, and then Dominick demanded Maria's attention again.

"I hope I'll run into you again sometime, Sara," said Maria as she piled an armful of pirate accessories by the cash register. "And think about what I said, OK?"

"What did she mean by that?" Katie asked curiously as she and Sara left the store.

"Oh, nothing interesting."

"Humph!" Katie snorted. "All right, I'll let you off the hook on that point if you tell me what you decided to dress up as," she bargained.

"And if I don't?"

"Then I'll—I'll burn all your Springsteen posters!" Katie raised one eyebrow ominously.

Sara dismissed Katie's threat with a scornful wave of her hand. "You could never bring yourself to do that, Katie Wilcox. You've had a crush on Bruce even longer than I have. But I'll tell you anyway, only because you're so great with clothes and all."

"Compliments will get you everywhere," Katie said with a grin. "So don't tell me—you're going to be a space cadet."

Sara giggled. "Not even close. I'm going to be a gypsy. Do you think that's a good idea? Not too unoriginal? Do you think Dave will like it?" Sara put special emphasis on the last question, but Katie didn't pick up on it.

"You know, I really think it is a good idea, kiddo," mused Katie, gazing thoughtfully at her friend as they headed toward the parking lot. "You're the perfect gypsy type, a dreamy-eyed Pisces."

"Have I just been insulted or complimented?"

"Complimented, definitely. Pisces are great people. Artistic, sensitive—sometimes a little *too* sensitive," she added meaningfully.

"I think I'll let that slide," said Sara, "if you'll help me with my costume."

"OK, chief. Here's my advice. Wear bright colors. They look the best with your dark skin. I've got this great pink peasant blouse you can borrow, and we can get some long ribbons from the fabric store and tie them up in your hair. By the time I'm through with you, the gypsy princes will be lining up outside your house waiting to carry you away."

"I don't want a gypsy prince, just Dave," Sara said wistfully.

"Well, you seem to be making pretty good progress to me," said Katie. "And after he sees you in your gorgeous, sexy costume you'll have him wrapped around your finger."

"He's used to going out with really beautiful girls, though." Sara was thinking of Julie Redman. Ever since she'd started to spend time with Dave, pictures of his "ex" seemed to be cluttering her mind like cobwebs.

"Unfortunately that's another Pisces characteristic." Katie sighed sorrowfully. "They're insecure."

Sara playfully swatted Katie with her canvas bag. "You'd better quit picking on me," she warned, only half joking. "I know only too well how insecure I am. You don't have to remind me."

"I'm not picking on you. I just want you to realize your own worth. Sure Julie Redman is pretty, but so are you, Sara. What reason could Dave have for dating you if he doesn't find you attractive?"

Sara shrugged. "I guess he does," she admitted. "But I don't want to take any chances on losing him. I've been dreaming about Dave Reiner for years, and finally my dreams are coming true. I still can't really believe it. You've got Jason, I don't think you really know how it feels to be without anyone."

Katie paused beside her car. "Of course I know how it feels not to have a boyfriend. I didn't always have Jason! The point is, Dave's lucky to have someone like you. You're worth a thousand Julie Redmans, and I'm not just saying that because I think she's a jerk."

Sara laughed out loud. "You can be my publicity agent any time," she said. "Maybe we can print an article in the *Star*: 'Dave Reiner counts his blessings.' "

Sara climbed into the little blue car as Katie started the engine. She'd definitely tell

Dave that she'd like to double with her friends. Katie would be really hurt if it didn't work out that way. Not that Dave could have any possible reason for objecting.

"Do you think Dave would want to go iceskating tomorrow? Jason mentioned something about going to the rink, and I thought you'd said you were going to be seeing Dave then, too."

"Oh, I'm sorry Katie, but Dave's planning on taking me to this show about fishing at the armory in Cheshire. He's into rods and reels and all that stuff," Sara explained.

Katie made a face, wrinkling her nose in distaste. "Doesn't sound like something you'd be interested in, though," she said, sounding surprised.

"Well, I'm trying to share some of his interests. Didn't you always say that's what I should do?" she asked.

Katie shrugged. "Caught by my own words. Well, if I said it, then it must be good advice. I just didn't realize what I'd be getting you into. I mean, *fishing*?"

"It can't be all that hard to learn how to catch fish. I'll just have to find some that'll take potato chips for bait," Sara said lightly. "Because I don't think that I could

ever bring myself to put a worm on a hook."
She shuddered.

"Just as long as you can hook Dave," said
Katie, her eyes gleaming mischievously.

Chapter Six

"Sara, it might be a good idea to put Abby outside before Dave gets here." Dr. Grant was sitting in the red leather easy chair that Sara and her mom had bought for him on his last birthday.

Sara sat cross-legged on the beige living room carpet, browsing through the Sunday paper looking at clothes. She had developed an avid interest in fashion since she'd started seeing Dave.

Abby lay sprawled out beside Sara, her eyes shut tightly and her breathing deep and even. Sara had spent an entire hour that morning trying to train her. It hadn't taken her long to realize that she should have worked harder with Abby when she was still a puppy. Obedience just wasn't going to come naturally to a full-grown Great Dane, especially a stubborn and spoiled one.

"I've been practicing 'sit' and 'stay' with Abby, and I think that she's finally gotten the idea," said Sara hopefully, putting the magazine aside.

"I'll believe that when I see it," Dr. Grant said wryly, tapping his pipe on the ashtray.

"OK, Dad, you asked for it." Sara accepted the challenge. "We'll show you what we can do." She jumped to her feet and whistled for Abby.

"Abby, come. Come on, girl!" She gave the hand signal for the Great Dane to come forward.

Abby stayed where she was, comfortably sprawled on the carpet. She did raise her head and turn it to the side, as if to question what Sara could possibly want with her.

"Abby, I said come," Sara insisted. She glanced at her father, who was trying unsuccessfully to stifle a smile, his blue eyes twinkling as he cleared his throat gruffly.

"Well, she listened this morning. I don't know why she's not obeying now," said Sara, standing over the dog. She slipped her hand through the leather collar and urged a surprised Abby to an upright position. "Come with me," she said firmly, as Abby stretched and stood up, then nuzzled her wet nose into Sara's side, begging for attention.

"You silly thing." Sara smiled and rubbed one of her ears. "I can never stay mad at you. You'd better behave yourself when Dave gets here." Sara tapped gently at Abby's nose just as the dog's tongue crept dangerously close to the plate of cheese and crackers at Dr. Grant's elbow. "I hope he'll be coming here a lot, and I don't want to have to lock you up all the time."

"Why don't you take Abby up with you?" Dr. Grant called as Sara headed toward the stairs. He needn't have bothered—Abby was right at Sara's heels.

"I just made the bed, so don't even think about getting on it," Sara warned Abby. She kicked off her slippers, ready to decide on the proper attire for a fishing equipment show.

Jeans were definitely in order. She opened her dresser drawer and pulled out a relatively new pair of jeans Katie had helped her pick out.

She tossed them onto the bed where they landed across Abby's back. The Great Dane had compromised and was lying half on and half off the twin bed.

Sara shook her head in resignation. "You're right, I *am* a pushover. Go ahead and stay where you are, you crazy dog."

She turned her attention back to the closet, pushing impatiently through her shirts. They were all too ordinary. She wanted to wear something extraspecial for her date with Dave, even if he'd probably be more captivated by the fishing rods than by her.

Then she remembered. She jumped for her dresser and yanked open the third drawer from the top. There was the beautiful sky blue cashmere sweater her mom had picked out for her sixteenth birthday.

Sara held the sweater up for inspection, gently rubbing its softness against her cheek. It would look good with jeans, she decided with satisfaction, dressing them up just enough.

She slipped off her pink flannel robe and began to dress.

She pulled on a pair of white ankle socks and folded down the tops. Her black loafers would be the perfect final touch, she thought, crawling into her closet to search for them. "I'm positive I left them right out in front— Abby, did you eat them?" Sara shrieked. "Oh, no, here they are. Sorry, dog, you were going to get blamed again." She sat on the edge of her bed and wiggled her feet into the loafers.

Sara flipped on her radio. Bruce Springsteen was playing the same song she'd heard with Dave in his Camaro. It would always remind her of their first date. It was practically their song.

A low growl reached Sara's ears even before the ring of the doorbell. Abby was off the bed like a shot and heading for the door.

"Wait a minute, dog. Hold it!" shouted Sara, trying to grab Abby's collar and ease her out the door. But before Sara could get a firm grasp, the dog charged out the door and down the stairs. Sara sprinted after Abby, no easy task considering that the soles on her loafers were still smooth and slippery and her feet were sliding all over the carpet.

"Mom, wait. *Don't* open the door." Sara grabbed the banister tightly and tottered down the stairs.

Mrs. Grant stood in the front hall, trying not to laugh. "Maybe we ought to put Abby out back until you and Dave leave," she suggested.

"I'll do it," offered Dr. Grant, taking hold of Abby's collar and leading her off with the promise of a dog biscuit.

The doorbell rang again. Sara felt herself

beginning to shake. She wanted everything to go perfectly that day, and now she was all flustered.

"How do I look?" she asked her mother as she peered into the hall mirror.

"Wonderful." Mrs. Grant smiled as she refastened one of the blue combs holding back Sara's tousled hair. "Your cheeks are a little flushed, but that just makes you look prettier."

Dr. Grant stuck his head back into the hall. "I think someone had better answer the door before your date leaves, pumpkin," he pointed out.

Sara steered herself around and turned the brass handle, pulling the door wide open. Every time she saw Dave he seemed handsomer than the time before. That day he was wearing a black turtleneck sweater, well-worn jeans, and a faded denim jacket. Sara thought he was better looking by far than any of the male models in the newspaper she'd just been reading.

As their eyes met and held, she was sure her heart actually stopped for a moment and then started up again at twice the normal rate. She'd have to ask her dad if this was a medically-recognized phenomenon.

Dave smiled, and his dimples deepened.

"You look fantastic, Sara," he said, running his eyes approvingly over her.

Sara felt her cheeks warm. *How embarrassing—I'm blushing,* she thought desperately. *Dave'll think I've never gotten a compliment from a boy before.*

"May I come in?" Dave asked. He was still standing in the doorway.

"Oh, sure. I'm sorry!" Sara hastily stepped aside to let him by. *That was a smooth move, Sara,* she chided herself. *You left him hanging outside on the steps while you were daydreaming.*

She led him into the living room where her parents were seated on the couch. Dr. Grant stood up to shake Dave's hand, and half a dozen sections of the Sunday paper showered to the floor around him. Sara gulped. "It's nice to meet you, Dave," he said warmly.

"It's nice to meet you, sir." Dave returned the handshake enthusiastically.

"Good to see you again," said Mrs. Grant, smiling. "We put the dog outside, so don't worry about getting trampled on this time."

Dave waved the idea aside. "That's OK. I really didn't mind," he said.

Sara turned to him in surprise. She couldn't believe he actually meant that. It had been obvious to her that Dave didn't care for dogs at all, let alone an overly demonstrative Great Dane. But he *looked* sincere. She probably ought to give him the benefit of the doubt.

"I understand you're a fisherman, Dave," said Dr. Grant, attempting to make conversation.

Dave nodded. "That's right. My father loves boats, and he's been taking me fishing ever since I was a little kid. We've got a thirty-foot cabin cruiser now," he said, warming to the subject.

"You must enjoy that. Last summer a friend and I went out on a fishing boat for the day, out on Long Island Sound, but it was awfully crowded and I'm afraid we didn't have much luck."

"I love going out on the boat, even if we don't catch anything," Dave said enthusiastically. "I usually sit up in the fly bridge and steer. You can get a great tan up there."

Sara had seen Dave around town over the summer and it was true, he had had an amazing tan. She wondered if maybe he'd invite her along on the boat the next summer. . . .

"By the way, Sara, I hate for us to run out like this, but the show's been on since this morning. If we don't leave pretty soon most of it will be over." Dave glanced pointedly at his watch, interrupting her thoughts.

"Oh. Sure, Dave. I'm ready," she said, reaching for her jacket.

As Dave and her parents said goodbye, Sara headed toward the front door. Her breath caught in her throat as she walked onto the brick step.

Dave had left the driver's door to the Camaro open, and Abby who loved riding in cars had made her best attempt to climb in. She was caught at an odd angle, three-quarters in the Camaro and one quarter out.

Sara ran up to the dog, who looked at her with an expectant expression as if to say: "If you give me a shove, I'll be ready to go."

"Abby, how did you get out of the backyard?" Sara hissed, putting both arms around the dog's neck and trying to haul her out of the front seat.

Abby was no help. She had her mind set on a ride in the car, and Sara couldn't budge her.

"What's going on?" Suddenly Dave was standing next to Sara in the driveway. "Why'd you let that stupid dog in my car?" he demanded, losing his temper.

Angry tears sprang to Sara's eyes. "First of all, I didn't *let* Abby in your car. Believe it or not, I'm doing my best to get her out. And second, she's not *stupid*. She just likes cars, that's all. I'd think *you'd* take that as a sign of intelligence." Sara finally managed to dislodge the Great Dane and pull her into the house.

When she came back to the car, Dave was brushing dog hair from his shiny black upholstery. Sara climbed into the car to help.

"I'm sorry if she made a mess," she said quietly, biting her lower lip. She could still feel tears burning behind her eyelids, but she was determined not to let Dave see them. She couldn't blubber and ruin their whole day together.

"No, *I'm* sorry," apologized Dave, sliding into his seat and pulling Sara close to him. "I shouldn't have yelled at you. It's just that I love this car, and I didn't expect to find a Great Dane in the front seat." He grinned. "I guess it's actually pretty funny! Wait'll I tell the guys about this—they'll probably get a real kick out of it," he said, starting the engine.

Sara's heart sank. *That's all I need to look like a real nerd in front of Dave's friends.* They wouldn't understand the way she felt about Abby.

Sara jumped when Dave took her hand.

"Hey, I had a brainstorm for the Halloween dance," he said, slipping a cassette in the tape deck. "I was watching MTV, and I got this incredible idea. It's a first-prize winner for sure."

Sara stared at him, not sure what to say.

"What do you think of punk rockers, kind of like we had our own band?" Dave grinned widely at himself in the rearview mirror. "We'll think up some really outrageous costumes, maybe even borrow a guitar from a friend of mine. It'll be great!" He nodded, clearly growing more and more thrilled with his idea.

The beautiful gypsy image faded sadly into Sara's imagination. *Goodbye, gold hoop earrings, hot pink eyelet blouse of Katie's, and all the rest of my dream,* she thought, swallowing hard to control her disappointment. Dave was obviously set on punkers, and she couldn't let him down, especially after what had just happened with the car.

"Well, what do you say, Sara? Or has my idea left you speechless?" He laughed, pleased with himself.

Sara managed a smile and tried her best to look excited. "It's great, Dave, really. We could get some ideas from magazines." *I might as well put in my two-cents worth,* she thought resignedly.

"Sure, or from watching MTV. You *do* have cable TV, don't you?" he asked.

"Umm, not yet. But my dad said we'll probably get it soon." Actually her father was only just considering the proposition. He was firmly convinced that the regular channels were enough and they should all watch less TV anyway. But Sara hadn't given up hope yet.

"Well, you can watch at my house, or I can tell you what some of the rock stars are wearing. Either way, it's in the bag," he said with satisfaction.

They drove not talking for a while, just listening to the radio. Finally Sara decided she had to mention doubling with her friends for the dance. She took a deep breath and dove in.

"Dave, I've been meaning to ask you something," she began hesitantly.

"Sure, Sara. Your wish is my command," he said with a grin.

She returned the smile. "My best friend, Katie Wilcox, asked us to double with her and her boyfriend for the dance. I promised her I'd ask you."

Dave pulled into a parking space in the armory lot, shut off the engine, and pocketed the key.

"Sara"—he turned in his seat to look directly at her—"I'd love to, but I already promised Chuck and Anita we'd be with them. I can't let them down now," he said with an apologetic shrug of his broad shoulders. "Come on, we are going to have one great day." He opened his car door and climbed out.

Sara felt as if someone had let all the air out of her balloon. Her day was not turning out as she had imagined it would. First there was Abby, then Dave had stamped out her gypsy idea, and now she would have to tell Katie she couldn't double with her.

She sighed as she followed Dave at a brisk pace across the parking lot, one of her black loafers skidding dangerously on a pebble. She decided not to touch anything at the show. With her luck she'd pick up the world's most expensive fishing rod and it would snap in two in her hands.

She needn't have worried. Most of the fishing equipment was safely mounted behind the glass display cases out of reach.

Dave was like a little boy let loose in a toy store at Christmas time. He stopped at a display, a bright smile lighting his face. "You see this fishing rod?" he asked Sara, pointing to a brown fiber glass fishing rod about six feet long.

Sara nodded in an attempt to be a good audience.

"That's the exact model my dad and I took camping with us when we went up to the lake to do some freshwater fishing. We have that spinning reel, too," he added, pointing toward a black reel also resting in the display case.

Try as she might, Sara couldn't exactly duplicate Dave's enthusiasm. One fishing rod looked pretty much like all the others to her, even though she'd have died before admitting it.

"Isn't that a dynamite rod?" Dave whistled admiringly.

Sara nodded once again. "It's beautiful," she agreed, not really knowing if that was a proper comment. But Dave didn't notice. He was on to the next display.

"I could use a new tackle box. I've had the same one since I was about twelve years old," he was saying thoughtfully. He stopped to open a large metal box with about a million compartments. Sara pretended to inspect it with a knowledgeable eye.

"Well, maybe next summer," Dave said, moving on as the dealer began closing up his display.

Sara followed along behind him, trying her

91

best to appear interested and ask intelligent questions—when she could get a word in edgewise, that is. She was relieved when the rest of the dealers began to close up and it was finally time to leave.

"I'm glad you liked the show," said Dave as she climbed into the car. "I guess it wouldn't appeal to all girls."

Sara smiled. It gave her a good feeling inside to know she had made Dave happy. Getting stuck looking at a bunch of dumb fishing rods for a couple of hours was a small price to pay for that. "It was very interesting. You taught me a lot," she said.

Dave reached for her hand. "Really?" he asked.

"Sure," she said, as Dave drew her close, slipping his arms around her waist. She could smell his after-shave—it was really exciting. Not many guys their age wore it, so it made Dave seem older.

Sara's eyes closed as his lips touched hers, and as usual she held her breath. Then he pulled away, and it took her a moment to open her eyes and drift back to reality.

So this is what it's like to be in love, Sara thought, staring at Dave's classic profile as he drove them home. It was wonderful but also scary and a little unsettling. Because deep down inside, Sara knew she was only pretending to share Dave's interests. And uncomfortable doubts nagged at her mind even though she tried her best to wish them away.

Chapter Seven

"Come on, you guys, help me lay this out flat on the floor. If I can't get the material to lay straight, the skeleton I paint will look like it's belly dancing!" Marsha said, struggling with a huge piece of black cloth.

"What would you do without us?" asked Katie as she helped her friend pull the fabric taut. The girls were continuing their decorations in the art room. Soon they'd be able to actually transform the gym.

"Do you really want me to answer that?" Marsha answered with a mischievous grin.

"No, what I really want is for our silent friend here to give us the details of her date with Prince Charming." Katie nodded toward

Sara, who was busily draping a white sheet over a form to look like a ghost.

"Maybe she's too busy with ghosts to think about Dave," suggested Marsha, opening a jar of white fluorescent paint.

Sara grinned to herself. She hadn't told her friends much about her date with David on Sunday. It had started out badly, but it had ended up terrifically well. She could still feel Dave's lips on hers if she closed her eyes. She shivered.

"Come on, Sara, quit holding out," ordered Marsha, wielding her paint brush in Sara's direction.

"Uh-oh, look at that smile on her face. Maybe the details are just too gruesome to share with even her very best friends." Katie's blue eyes sparkled devilishly.

"All right, you guys, cut it out. There's really not that much to tell!"

"Oh, I'll bet." Marsha dabbed at her skeleton. "You go out with one of the best-looking guys at Stanford High, and then there's nothing to tell. Sounds to me like there might be a little too much to tell."

"Wait, Marsha. Maybe Sara's right," Katie declared. "If she wants to keep her personal life private, then that's totally up to her. Just because *I* confide *everything* in you guys doesn't mean Sara has to do the same."

Marsha caught Katie's wink and winked back. "That's true," she said. "And just because I was thrilled to tell you when Rick Davenport asked me to the dance, providing generous details of how he looked and what he said and what I said back, that's no reason for Sara to have to share the details of her date with us."

"OK, OK, you win!" Sara threw the sheet up in defeat. She did want to tell her friends about her date with Dave, but for some reason she felt a little nervous talking about him. It was funny—it was almost as if she were afraid that if she thought about it or talked about it too much she might suddenly find out that it had all been a mistake: Dave wasn't really interested in her at all. She didn't want to wake up and find out that it had all been just another dream.

The real problem was, she didn't know how to tell them she and Dave would be going to the dance with Chuck and Anita. She knew that she could still try to spend part of the time with her own friends, but the fact was that Dave had made other plans. And that bothered Sara, more than just a little. Once again he'd made a decision that concerned them both without even consulting her.

"Well, part of what I've got to tell you isn't too great," she admitted.

"Don't tell me you and Dave are having trouble already." Katie was instantly sympathetic.

Sara shook her head. "No, it's not that. But I'm afraid we won't be able to double with you guys to the dance."

Marsha and Katie exchanged glances.

"But we've been planning on it." Katie sounded hurt. "Why can't we?"

Sara shrugged. "I don't know. I asked Dave about it, but he said he'd already made plans with Anita and Chuck. You know that I'd rather be with you guys," she added quickly, seeing how upset her friends were.

"Oh, Sara, we were all counting on it," Marsha said, her gray eyes wide and troubled. She turned back to her painting. Sara felt terrible.

"Listen, I'm sure we'll still run into each other a lot at the dance," she reasoned feebly.

"Why didn't you try telling Dave to ask you *first before* doing something like that?" asked Katie quietly, twisting the ends of her long blond hair around her finger.

"I'm afraid to," admitted Sara. "You were

always the one who told me to go along with whatever the guy wants to do. And you were right. It's been working perfectly up till now, but I might lose him if I stop."

"Sara, you forgot one very important word," said Katie. "I said *sometimes.* Do the things the boy likes to do *sometimes.* Not *all* the time. You're becoming so absorbed in trying to anticipate what Dave wants that you're not yourself anymore."

"That's not true," Sara said defensively. "I'm still me, it's just that I've got a boyfriend now, and I have to consider his feelings, too."

"Maybe you worry about him a little too much," offered Marsha. "You spend so much time tutoring him after school we hardly ever get together anymore. Are you sure Dave appreciates everything you do for him anyway?"

"Of course he does!" Sara pushed back her thick hair angrily. She didn't like her friends picking on Dave like that. They had no right to ruin all her good feelings.

And she was just following their advice! Well, maybe their advice worked too well. *Maybe they're just jealous,* she decided.

She went back to pinning and draping the ghost, and she pricked her finger. "Ouch!" Sara felt hot tears running down her cheeks.

Katie and Marsha turned to her in concern, but she just couldn't face them anymore.

"I've got to run," she mumbled, grabbing her books and running out of the art room before they could say anything to stop her.

Sara wiped her nose as she walked down the empty hallway. She could understand her friends' disappointment about not going to the dance together. She was disappointed, too. But if Dave had already promised his friends, she supposed she could understand his side of it, too.

All she had ever wanted was a boyfriend, like everybody else. She just hadn't realized all the complications that would come along with one.

Sara glanced at her watch. She and Marsha and Katie had been excused from the last period of the day so they could work on the decorations. Since there were only ten minutes left in the school day, she decided she might as well go home a few minutes early.

She headed for her locker. She needed to pick up her math book to study for a test she had first period in the morning. Math was not her strongest subject—she had to put in a lot of studying time to do well on the exams.

"Hey, Sara, just the person I was looking for!"

Sara's pulse quickened, and her mouth went as dry as cotton. She was still amazed by the physical reaction Dave had on her. She forgot all about the argument she had just had with Marsha and Katie.

"Hi, Dave!" She tingled all over at the thought that he had been looking for her.

"I checked your schedule in the office, and you were supposed to be in study hall last period," he said. "I tried there, but I couldn't find you."

"I was working in the art room trying to finish up the decorations for the dance," she explained.

"That's OK, as long as I found you now," he said with the smile that melted Sara's heart. He took her hand and swung it back and forth. "You could do me one enormous favor."

Sara waited breathlessly.

"I promised my sister I'd drive her to dance class this afternoon. My mother's busy, and otherwise she'll miss her lesson." His hand squeezed hers tightly.

"How can I help you, Dave?" she asked, puzzled.

"Well, I forgot all about the Student Activities Council meeting after school today. I can't be in two places at the same time, can I?"

"I can cover the meeting for you," Sara said eagerly.

"Sara, you are a lifesaver," cried Dave, grabbing her in a bear hug and swinging her around the corridor. "You're really terrific." His lips brushed hers in a brief kiss.

Sara was sure he could hear her heart pounding; it sounded a lot like the Stanford High marching band at half time. Dave was definitely the neatest guy in the whole world. She was really beginning to believe he cared about her as much as she cared about him.

"Where's the meeting?" she asked, trying to sound nonchalant.

"Room Two-oh-six. I'll walk you over and introduce you around," he said, still holding her hand.

Sara couldn't remember ever having been that happy before.

"Here we are." Dave pushed the door open with his shoulders.

The classroom was empty except for a tall, sandy-haired boy going over some papers at the front desk.

"Hey—Chris, my man. I want to introduce you to the sweetest girl at Stanford High," said Dave, slapping the other boy heartily on the back.

The boy turned around with a shy smile.

His eyes were partially hidden behind gold wire-rimmed glasses, but Sara could still see that they were dark brown and very friendly.

"It's nice to meet you," he said, extending his hand to Sara shaking it firmly.

"I'm Chris Forrester."

"Sara Grant. It's nice to meet you, too," she said sincerely.

"OK, great. Now that you two guys know each other, I've got to take off." Dave tousled her hair and headed for the door. "Sara, all you have to do is take notes on the meeting. I'll stop by your house tomorrow morning and pick you up for school. I want to go over some ideas for costumes with you anyway."

"That'll be great," Sara called after him, waving until he was out of sight.

"That's some guy," said Chris in an odd tone as the door closed behind Dave.

"I know," agreed Sara with a huge sigh.

Chris gave her a sort of funny look, but Sara chalked it up to her imagination. That day had been such a mixed-up day.

"So you're going to fill in for Dave today."

Sara nodded. "Yes, he had to drive his sister somewhere, but he's still responsible for an article getting in the paper. I'm actually looking forward to it."

Chris ran a hand through his sandy blond

hair, making it stand on end, which Sara thought looked kind of cute. "Why? Are you interested in the Activities Council?" he asked, sounding surprised.

"Yes, I am. I wanted to run this year, but I'm not really the type to campaign in an election or anything. I guess I'm kind of shy."

Somehow Chris made it easy for her to confess this. He smiled warmly. "You don't seem very shy to me," he observed. "And besides, you don't have to run for an office to be involved with the council. Only the officers have to be elected."

"You're kidding! I guess I should have known that." Sara was thinking about Chris saying she didn't seem shy. Actually, he was right. She did feel as if she was coming out of her shell lately. But then she supposed Dave had a lot to do with that. Knowing that he liked her made her feel more important, as though she had more to offer the world.

Sara realized she was still holding Chris's gaze, but somehow she couldn't tear her own eyes away. He was really kind of good-looking, she decided suddenly.

Then she felt guilty for having had such a disloyal thought. How could she think that another boy was cute when she was dating Dave?

M.W.—6

"You know, Sara, you're welcome to join the council even now. The Halloween Dance is only our first big event of the year. We're planning a fund-raising drive to feed the needy at Thanksgiving, and we'll have a lot of things going on around Christmas."

Sara found herself growing excited about the upcoming events. Chris's enthusiasm was catching. Maybe she would join the committee—if she could make the time. She was so busy with Dave right then that she didn't know if she had any room in her schedule.

"Why don't you see how you feel about it after the meeting," suggested Chris, noticing Sara's look of indecision.

"That's a good idea," Sara said. *If the other kids are all as friendly as you, I won't be able to resist joining,* she added to herself.

She slipped into a seat, and Chris introduced her around as the others filed in. Everyone smiled and welcomed her enthusiastically. Sara found herself wondering why she would even hesitate to get involved. She could tell she was really going to enjoy getting to know these people and making plans for school activities.

"OK," began Chris, standing at the front of the room to bring the meeting to order. "Sara Grant is taking notes for the *Star* today, and

I'll start with an update on the dance. I think just about everything has already been taken care of—we've got decorations all over the school. I peeked in the art room earlier this afternoon and really thought the decorations are looking great." He winked at Sara. "Definitely gruesome."

"The decorating committee has done a terrific job so far," said Chris, looking directly at Sara. "We have one member right here with us, so let's give her a hand."

Sara blushed as everyone turned to look at her. There was a spattering of applause and a few whistles.

"I guess that's one committee you didn't mind joining, huh?" said Chris.

"OK. The refreshment people have the menu all planned, and we've even managed to assemble a clean-up committee. Can you believe it? So we're in great shape for the dance, and I for one am psyched."

Chris placed a sheet of paper face down on the desk and picked up the next one. "Now, for the fund-raising drive. Someone suggested a bake sale, but we had one last spring. Are there any other ideas?" he asked, throwing the floor open for suggestions.

"How about a big rummage sale?" suggested Sara, surprising herself. "You know, we could put flyers up all over the school asking for donations, and we could have a big spread in the *Star* about it, too. Everyone has something at home they'd like to get rid of."

"I think that's a terrific idea," said Chris enthusiastically. "How many of you guys are in favor?"

Everyone in the room raised their hands. Sara's face flushed with excitement. They loved her idea! And she knew she must look as triumphant and confident as she felt. This was great. It really was lucky that Dave had to take his sister to dance class—this meeting was opening up a whole new world to her.

Chapter Eight

"Sara, you've got exactly two minutes until the school bus comes." Mrs. Grant's voice floated urgently up the stairs.

"It's OK, Mom. Dave's picking me up this morning," called Sara from her desk, where she was scrambling to find the notes she'd taken at the meeting and rewritten last night.

She had had such a good time sitting in with the Activities Council. Once she had come up with the idea for the rummage sale everyone had become involved, tossing suggestions back and forth, debating various advertising methods. Best of all, she had been congratulated over and over again on her wonderful idea. Everyone had been happy to give her credit and be appreciative of her input.

She had been especially proud of Chris's response. He'd stopped her for a moment after the meeting to tell her how glad he was she had attended, and how important her presence had been. He had urged her to join the group, and she had promised to give him an answer soon.

She knew she wanted to join. That wasn't the problem. But she had her schoolwork, and she had gotten so involved with tutoring Dave that she didn't have much time left for herself or her friends. Still, the committee looked like a lot of fun. Maybe she would talk it over with Dave that morning, she thought, slipping the draft of the article into her bag. Maybe he didn't need to be tutored as much.

She heard the double blast of a car horn and leaned on the windowsill so that she could see out more easily.

Dave's red Camaro was parked in the driveway, and he was still seated behind the steering wheel. As he beeped the horn again, Sara grabbed her bag and flew down the stairs. It was obvious from her mother's expression that she didn't exactly approve of Dave's method of calling her daughter.

"I guess he's running late, Mom," said Sara

as she flung open the front door and ran down the brick walk. "Bye!" *Or maybe he just doesn't want to have another close encounter with Abby,* she thought to herself with a big giggle.

"Hey, Sara!" Dave called with a bright smile, throwing open the passenger door for her.

She climbed into the car. "Hi, Dave," she said. Before she knew it he was pulling her to him for a brisk good-morning kiss. His lips met hers for half a second and then he refocused on his car.

"How'd the meeting go?" he asked, looking over his shoulder as he pulled out of the driveway and onto the road.

"Great." Sara reached into her canvas bag for the bundle of notes.

"They look fantastic. You didn't have to type them up, but I'm glad you did," said Dave, glancing at the neatly typewritten pages while they stopped at a traffic light.

"I didn't mind," said Sara, proud that she had done such a good job. "I really liked going to the meeting. I'm even considering joining the committee," she added, hoping Dave would approve of the idea.

He remained silent, his eyes glued to the road. Sara felt nervous, and then a little bit irritated. What reason could he have for objecting?

"Don't you think that's a good idea?" she asked hesitantly.

Dave shrugged. "It's not that, Sara." He flashed her a heart-stopping smile. "It's just that you did such a great job on these notes, I was thinking you might cover some of the other meetings for me, too. That might be a little tricky if you were a regular member," he explained. "Kind of like a conflict of interests."

Sara didn't know what to say. If Dave really needed her to help him out with his newspaper work, then she didn't want to let him down. But she'd really had her heart set on joining the Activities Council, and she had a feeling that Chris Forrester was counting on her.

Dave seemed to read her mind. "It's not like you wouldn't be at the meetings. You could go to as many as you like—as my assistant," he said, reaching for her hand.

His hand was so warm around her cold one. It really was something else to be this close to Dave, a boy whom for so long she had only been able to admire from a distance.

"Listen, Sara, you do whatever you want. If you'd rather join the council than go as my assistant, then I'll just have to try and make the time myself. Or maybe I can get someone else to help me out."

"No, I don't want you to do that, Dave," she said quickly. "Of course I'll go for you, whenever you need me to."

Dave rewarded her with another smile. "I knew I could count on you, Sara. You're one in a million."

Once they were parked in the school lot, he took her in his arms. Sara felt dizzy. She pressed her hot face against the cool leather of his jacket. She knew her heart was going haywire. When Dave kissed her, she had the strangest sensation that she was caught up in a strong current and being carried far away. It was exciting, but there was also something about the feeling that made her uncomfortable; and it didn't go away until Dave left her inside the heavy wooden doors of the school building.

Sara stood lost in thought as she watched him stride down the corridor, her hands buried deep in the pockets of her hunter green wool jumper. Then the bell rang and she hurried to her first class—math. Just as she took her seat she remembered her big test was that morning. The test she had meant to study for the night before but had slipped her mind while she concentrated on revising and typing the notes for Dave's article.

Sara felt sick. Mr. Levinson handed out the test papers, then took his seat in front of the room. She watched her classmates take out calculators and pencils and bend their heads over their exams.

She hadn't even remembered to bring her calculator that day, she had been in such a hurry to meet Dave. It was one exam she had a feeling she'd never forget.

Sara pushed her tray along the line in the cafeteria. Pizza was the daily special, and it actually looked good, but she was sure whatever she ate would taste like sawdust after the morning she had just been through. The math exam had been a nightmare.

She decided on a tossed salad and a piece of chocolate layer cake and moved along to the cashier's.

"Nice lunch," came a male voice from behind her in the line.

Sara looked back into a pair of laughing brown eyes. "Chris, hi!" It made her feel so good to see him that she forgot all about her problems.

"That's no meal for a growing girl," he said sternly, nodding toward her tray.

"Gee Dad, I guess it is kind of strange," she admitted with a grin. "But I'm in a kind of strange mood."

"Still reeling from the excitement of the meeting yesterday, huh?" While Sara ransacked her canvas bag for the five-dollar bill she was sure she'd tossed in there this morning, Chris paid for both their lunches.

"Thanks, Chris," said Sara, surprised and pleased. "If I'd known you were treating I would have ordered the filet mignon."

"I'll make you a deal, Sara," promised Chris. "The day that Stanford High puts filet mignon on their menu, I'll take you to lunch again."

They both laughed, standing together awkwardly, neither one moving toward a table.

"By the way," said Sara sincerely, "I really enjoyed that meeting. You guys get a lot accomplished."

Chris nodded in agreement. "I think we did yesterday, and a lot of that was due to you. I hope you've decided to join us. You did promise to think it over."

Sara hesitated, unsure of how to phrase her answer.

"Why don't we grab a table over there?" Chris moved toward an empty table in the corner.

Sara followed him, sliding her dishes off the tray and taking the seat beside his.

"I did think it over," she began, avoiding his eyes.

"I think I hear a 'but' coming," observed Chris as he picked up a steaming slice of pizza. A long strand of cheese still connected it to the plate and he moved the pizza up and down making the cheese stretch like a rubber band.

Sara giggled, then shrugged regretfully. "The 'but' is that Dave needs me to help him with his column. If I go to the meetings to take notes for the *Star,* I can't really participate fully," she explained, pushing her salad around the plate with her fork.

"But why do you have to take all the notes for Dave?" Chris asked. "You're not on the *Star* staff."

Sara speared a cherry tomato. "I know, but he's kind of bogged down with a lot of work lately. He's having some trouble in Spanish." Sara was a little embarrassed to be making excuses—and such lame ones at that. Besides, it really wasn't Chris's business to know anything about her relationship with Dave.

But somehow Sara didn't resent Chris's interest. Because it *was* interest. She knew he wasn't just being nosy. He genuinely liked her, and she liked him, too.

Chris turned on the bench so that he was facing Sara. "I'm sorry, Sara. I didn't mean to put you on the spot about Dave. I just hate to see the council lose you as a potential member," he said regretfully.

Sara studied his face. Chris looked like a high school version of the classic absent-minded professor, complete with wayward hair and crazy glasses. *Very* cute.

"Maybe I can come to the next meeting. I'm sure that Dave won't mind," she compromised.

"I'm sure he won't mind, either." Chris turned his attention back to his lunch.

Sara was wondering what he meant by that remark when they were joined by the subject of their conversation.

"Hey, what did I start by introducing you two?" Dave asked, sliding in beside Sara and surprising her.

Sara blushed. "Don't look so guilty, Sara," said Chris. "It'd do this guy some good to have a little honest competition."

"We were just having lunch," explained Sara, suddenly not hungry at all.

"I was only kidding, Sara. I know I can trust you." Dave grinned, squeezing her arm possessively. "I just dropped by to give you something. I meant to show you this in the car this morning, but we got sidetracked," he said with a meaningful look.

Sara avoided looking in Chris's direction and concentrated on the sheet of paper David handed her. It was a page torn from a rock magazine, a photograph of a female rock star wearing a sexy outfit that was *very* revealing.

"I thought you might want to wear something like this for the costume dance," said Dave.

"Dave, you have to be joking," Sara gasped.

"Why?" he asked, his blue eyes wide and innocent. "Your figure is every bit as good as Madonna's, maybe even better." He looked at her approvingly.

Chris glanced at the picture and raised his eyebrows.

"I mean you could tone it down a little," Dave conceded reluctantly. "But this'll give you a general idea. I've already got my outfit all planned out. A leather belt with metal studs, boots, the whole bit."

Sara was beginning to regret her decision to go along with Dave's punk rocker scheme. To say that a female rock star wasn't her style was the understatement of the year. She'd really need Katie and Marsha to help her with this one. If they were still speaking to her, that is.

"Listen, I've got to run. Keep the picture." Dave bent to drop a kiss on the top of her head.

"Catch you later," he called to Chris as he hurried out of the cafeteria. "I've got a great article for this week's *Star*."

"Thanks to you-know-who." Chris winked, but Sara just shook her head. She didn't know what to think about Dave or Chris or anything. She felt backed into a corner and wasn't at all sure she'd ever be able to find her way out again.

"Need a ride home?" called a familiar voice as Sara sat on the concrete steps at the side door of the school building waiting for the bus.

Marsha's yellow VW was a sight for sore eyes. Katie turned around in the front seat and unlocked the back door and pushed it open for Sara.

"Just call us your friendly, Tuesday-afternoon taxi service," said Marsha with a welcoming smile.

"You don't know how glad I am to see you guys," said Sara, climbing in and settling back gratefully.

"Sorry I missed you at lunch today, but I had a bit of work to finish in the art room," said Marsha as she headed out of the school parking lot.

"I wasn't there, either. There was a special meeting of the drama club," said Katie. "I hope you didn't have to eat alone, Sara."

"I saw Dave at lunch today," began Sara. She decided not to mention her encounter with Chris. She wanted to make up with her friends, not lead them to think she was interested in another boy. That would just complicate their lives further.

"You seem to be pretty serious about him," observed Katie, turning around in her seat to face Sara.

"I am." Sara nodded, meeting her friend's eyes. "And I really need your help with my costume for the dance," she added.

"I thought that Dave had decided you should both go as rock stars."

"We are, but there are rock stars and then there are rock stars." Sara unfolded the pictures Dave had given her. "Dave thinks I should dress something like this." She passed the picture up to the front seat. "But I'm not convinced."

Marsha burst out laughing, and Katie hooted.

"Go ahead, make fun of me," Sara said good-naturedly.

"I'm sorry, Sara, it's just too funny," Marsha apologized.

"I'd say that you were more the Shirley Temple type." Katie's blue eyes twinkled.

"I really don't think that Shirley Temple would be considered a rocker," observed Sara.

"Well, maybe we can compromise," suggested Marsha.

Sara sighed. "I guess you're right. What I need to find are two mismatched sneakers and a pair of hot-pink tights." The three girls burst into laughter.

"That purple jacket is too much!"

The girls were dressing for the costume dance in Sara's room, and Katie had brought over a huge white shopping bag full of outrageous accessories.

"Believe it or not, I found it at the Thrift Shop for the Visiting Nurse Association," said Katie, reaching into the bag and pulling out one purple sneaker and one green one. "Compliments of the thrift shop again, and my big brother Steven." She tossed them onto the carpet.

"You're the greatest, Katie," said Sara gratefully as she pulled on a pair of lime-green ankle socks over her hot-pink tights. "You don't think these colors are a little too loud, do you?" she asked doubtfully.

"Are you kidding? Rockers aren't exactly shy," said Marsha, squinting into the mirror as she plastered on the white face paint she was using as a base for her clown makeup.

"Well, even if we can't go together, it's fun getting dressed together." Katie straightened the seam in her textured stockings. She was wearing a brightly flowered sixties-style mini-skirt, a lemon-yellow stretch top, several strands of psychedelic love beads, and a pair of white vinyl go-go boots.

"You know, you look absolutely fantastic," said Sara, admiring Katie's costume.

"You really do," agreed Marsha. Her voice sounded strange coming through a round red rubber nose. "I don't know why the rest of us are even bothering. You'll win for sure."

Katie smiled. "Don't be ridiculous," she said, waving aside the compliments. "These are just some old things I threw together for fun. You two are really going all out."

"Here." She held out the jacket as Sara slipped it on over a sleeveless green tank top. The oversize purple jacket was practically the same length as the pink miniskirt she wore.

"I look weird, all right," said Sara, pushing

back the sleeves of the jacket and putting on the assortment of bracelets her friends had gathered.

"It's just a shame your date isn't Hulk Hogan or you'd win for sure." Katie laughed, leaning back on the bed to survey her friend.

"Thanks, but no thanks. I'm happy to be going with Dave," said Sara firmly. "Are you sure this looks OK?" She brushed her hair to one side and began cautiously spraying it with the bright orange coloring Katie had promised would wash out.

"Perfect," murmured Marsha as she applied red clown makeup around her mouth in a huge grin. "There, now I'll be smiling all night long."

"I think we all look great," declared Katie. "Even Abby. She could go to the dance as a dog and win first prize for the most realistic costume, since she thinks she's a person in real life."

"I don't think Dave would appreciate that." Sara smiled ruefully. "He and Abby aren't exactly the best of friends."

"That's too bad, but I guess it doesn't matter as long as you and Dave get along, right?" Marsha stuffed a pillow into the stomach of her costume.

Sara nodded. "Yes, the only thing that's

important is that Dave and I get along just great."

"Shoot, it's almost seven o'clock! We'd better get out of here, Marsha. Dave'll be here to pick Sara up any minute, and Jason and Rick will be at my house by seven-thirty for sure," cried Katie, gathering up her makeup and throwing it all into the white shopping bag.

"How did it get so late so fast?" wondered Marsha, adding tubes of greasepaint to the clutter.

"We'll see you at the dance," promised Katie, squeezing Sara's hand in excitement.

Sara leaned on the windowsill, watching as her friends climbed into Marsha's VW and pulled out of the driveway. She really hoped she'd be able to spend some time with them once she and Dave got to the dance. It would be such a drag if she had to hang out with Anita all night. Sara had seen her around school since that night at the movies, but she was never friendly—unless Dave was around of course. Then she gushed all over the place as if Sara were her best friend.

Sara knew that Anita's best friend was Julie Redman, and she always got the feeling that the two of them were whispering about her. *I'm probably just paranoid*, she told herself as she heard the distinctive roar of Dave's car.

"Well, here I go, Abby. Trick or treat."

The Great Dane galloped to the window and pressed her nose against the pane. Spotting Dave, she spun excitedly in a circle with her usual deep welcoming barks. She was all set to follow Sara downstairs to greet the company.

"Sorry, pal, but you've got to stay up here." Sara closed the bedroom door firmly behind her.

Dave was sitting on the living room couch, helping Sara's father adjust the light meter on his camera. He gave a long, low whistle as Sara entered the room.

"Hel-lo, rocker," he said with an approving smile.

"Do you really like it?" she asked, pleased with his reaction.

"I love it! You're going to have the best costume there," he said with assurance.

"Aside from yours," said Sara. Dave had really gone all out. He wore a pair of skin-tight, tattered jeans, a body-hugging sleeveless T-shirt that showed off his muscled chest, and a black leather jacket. Around his waist was a wide black belt with shiny metal studs, and dozens of chains dangled from his neck.

M.W.—7

His hair stood up in spikes. The finishing touch was a single rhinestone earring. He really did look as if he'd just stepped out of an MTV video.

"Your mother insists that I take a picture of you two," said Dr. Grant, focusing the camera.

Dave put his arm around Sara's waist and drew her close. Mrs. Grant watched from the couch.

"I hate to sound out of it, but what ever happened to dressing as witches and ghosts for Halloween?" she asked, shaking her head.

"Oh, Mom, we're not six years old anymore!" Sara wished her mother would stop treating her like a baby, especially in front of Dave.

"There, I've got it." Dr. Grant put the camera down on the coffee table.

"Do you think I could get an extra print when you have it developed?" asked Dave.

"I'll be sure to make you one," promised Dr. Grant. "And if you win the contest, I'll make it an eight-by-ten glossy," he added with a smile

"But there'll be so many other great costumes," said Sara. "Wait until you see Katie and Marsha, Dave. They look absolutely fantastic."

"Maybe," he said. "But I still think that

we've got it in the bag." He turned toward the front door.

"Well, I think we'd better get going, Sara."

Sara nodded in agreement. "Don't wait up," she told her parents, knowing that they would.

"I'll be up late tonight doing some paperwork for the office, anyway," said Mrs. Grant with a smile.

Sara smiled back. She might have expected that to be her mother's answer. Mrs. Grant never went to sleep until she knew that Sara was safely in the house.

"Have a wonderful time," called Dr. Grant.

"We will," promised Dave, squeezing Sara's hand as they said their goodbyes and walked out into the crisp October night.

"We *are* going to have a fantastic time tonight," Dave said, squeezing her hand for emphasis. "I told Chuck and Anita we'd meet them at the refreshment table. The gym will be mobbed, and I don't want to miss them."

Sara's heart sank. She wouldn't mind "missing" Chuck and Anita at all, then she'd be able to hunt up her own friends. Well, maybe Dave would forget about them after they were at the dance for a while.

The high school parking lot was bumper to bumper with cars, and it seemed as though the entire school had turned out for the dance.

As the wide double doors to the school lobby opened and closed, loud rock music echoed out into the still night air.

"It sounds as though the school's really alive," said Dave, maneuvering into a parking space and shutting off the engine. "Are you ready?" His blue eyes glittered with excitement.

Sara smiled. He looked like a little boy about to go to his first party. "Sure," she said, hoping that that night would be a night she would always remember.

It was almost impossible for Dave to walk two feet without someone shouting out a greeting or slapping him on the back. Everyone wanted his attention. It took them almost twenty minutes just to get inside the gym, and then another ten to push through the crowd to get to the refreshment table.

"Where have you guys been?" asked Chuck. He was dressed as a football jock, not really much of a costume since that was what he really was, thought Sara. Anita was dressed in her cheerleader's uniform—even more original.

"It's like an oven in here," complained Anita, fanning herself with a paper plate. "Grab some punch while you still can," she advised.

Dave elbowed his way to the front of the refreshment line.

"Hey, look who's manning the punch bowl!" he cried. "Chris, my man, don't tell me you came to this bash stag."

Sara was embarrassed for Chris, whose face reddened as he ladled punch into paper cups for them.

"It's a dirty job but someone had to do it," he said. "Jennifer and I don't mind. We get first shot at all the cookies and brownies."

Sara recognized the pretty blond girl from the Student Activities Council meeting. Maybe Chris wasn't there stag after all. He and Jennifer probably came to the dance together. Sara was surprised by the pang of disappointment she felt at the idea that Chris might be dating someone.

"Well, it might not be so bad with a pretty little Indian squaw like that standing next to you." Dave checked out Jennifer's brown suede Indian costume with a practiced eye.

Chris was dressed as a doctor in a baggy green operating-room shirt and pants, a stethoscope and mask hanging around his neck.

"That's an interesting costume," said Sara, sipping the punch he had handed her.

"Just a peek at the future. I'm thinking of

being a veterinarian." He smiled with amusement at her outfit. "And you're going to be a rock star, right?"

Sara shook her head. "Not quite! Actually I should be dressed more like you. I don't know if I'd want to be a vet, but I'd love to work with animals. If I ever open a kennel, you can pay the house calls."

"So rock 'n' roll isn't the real you, huh?" Sara thought she read approval in his eyes. "By the way, you did a great job decorating this place." Chris nodded toward the floating white ghosts and shimmering skeletons that hovered in all the dim corners of the room.

Sara was about to answer when Dave grabbed her arm and propelled her toward the crowded dance floor, abruptly ending her conversation with Chris. "Come on, let's dance!"

The music was so loud that it was impossible to talk, so she and Dave just concentrated on dancing. They stomped energetically, first to the Rolling Stones, then to Tina Turner, then to Duran-Duran. Sara was exhausted when it was finally announced that the judges would begin handing out the best-costume awards.

"Come on, let's get front-row seats for this." Dave directed Sara toward the little orange-and-black stage that had been set up at one end of the gym. She was beginning to feel like a puppet—Dave pulled the strings, and she went along with him.

Sara was surprised to see Chris Forrester standing at the podium, microphone in hand. "As president of the Student Activities Council, I have the exciting job of announcing the winners of the costume contest," he said, raising his hand to quiet the room. "The judges had a really hard time choosing because there are a lot of great costumes here tonight."

"Come on, Forrester, get on with it," called Chuck, clapping his hands together loudly.

Chris continued as if he hadn't heard the interruption. "Second prize goes to Kyle Warrington as Santa Claus and Julie Redman as a Christmas elf!" he announced.

Sara felt Dave stiffen as Julie and her date pushed their way through the cheering crowd to accept their awards. Kyle was wearing a full Santa Claus suit. And Julie wore a strapless green bathing suit, with white puffy trim. Her thick red hair was loose under her elf hat, and her long legs seemed to go on forever as she tottered up to the stage in matching green heels.

She accepted the prize with a wide, practiced smile, kissing first Chris's cheek and then Kyle's before she left the stage amid a thunder of applause and whistles.

Julie didn't have much of a costume, thought Sara wryly. She tried to ignore a nagging feeling of insecurity and irritation prompted by Dave's obvious awareness of Julie.

"And now for our first-prize winners." Chris paused for effect. "Dave Reiner and Sara Grant as our very own punk rockers." he cried, clapping his hands enthusiastically.

Sara couldn't believe she had actually heard her own name. She was sure there must have been some mistake. Dave literally had to lift her onstage to accept their prize.

When Chris reached out to kiss Sara's cheek, he whispered warmly "Good going, kid. You really deserve this."

Sara was so excited she was shaking. All she wanted was to get off the stage before she made a fool of herself and embarrassed Dave.

But Dave was in his element, oblivious of everything but his own enormous satisfaction. He was grinning from ear to ear, raising his fists above his head in a gesture of triumph to his many friends in the crowd.

"Way to go, Reiner," called a voice, and the rest followed with loud cheers of approval.

Sara was a little uncomfortable by the way

Dave was flaunting his own victory. They had had their moment in the spotlight, but he just didn't seem to want it to end. She spotted Katie and Jason waving frantically to her. She knew a good part of the prize belonged to her friends for helping her put her costume together. It gave her a happy feeling to know that they were there rooting for her.

A slow song was being played, and Dave ushered her out onto the dance floor. "Do you think we could stop by and talk to my friends for a minute?" she asked.

"Hey, they're playing this song for us." Dave didn't give her a chance to protest. He pressed his body close to hers, his arms locked firmly around her. *I might as well be out with Hulk Hogan*, thought Sara for a second. *This sure feels like a wrestling move.*

The lights dimmed, and the room was hushed. The music was romantic, and Dave *was* the most impressive date any girl could ask for. Sara knew she had gotten her wish. It would be a night she would always remember. But maybe not for the reason she'd expected. Out of the corner of her eye she could see Chris dancing cheek to cheek with Jennifer. She couldn't tear her gaze away, any more than she could dismiss the feeling for Chris that was blossoming inside her.

Chapter Nine

"What do they call a spy in China?" Jason's hazel eyes twinkled expectantly.

He sat across the lunch table from Katie and Sara, who exchanged exaggerated looks of pain.

"I don't think I'm ready for one of your riddles, this early on a Monday," said Katie, rolling her blue eyes toward the ceiling of the cafeteria.

"Oh, come on, you know you adore my unique sense of humor," said Jason.

"Well, I'll listen—only because I'm such a good sport, not to mention a wonderful person," she said, wrapping her fingers around his.

"OK. Do *you* have an answer, Miss Star of the costume dance?" he asked Sara.

Sara sighed. She was proud of winning first prize, especially since it had made Dave so happy. That was all he talked about—what a great team they made, and how he knew he could always count on her. But in her heart she knew the contest hadn't been all that important. And secretly she had believed Katie's sixties costume was better than her own, and certainly better than Julie Redman's costume.

"Actually, I forgot the question," she admitted.

"What an audience," groaned Jason. "What do they call a spy in China?" he repeated.

Katie shook her head.

"A Peking Tom," announced Jason. He slapped his hand on the table and laughed.

Katie shook her head. "I guess that does pass for a unique sense of humor. Anybody else would be afraid to tell a joke that bad!"

"Oh, yeah?" Jason pretended to be hurt.

"That was even worse than the joke *we* used to tell in third grade," Sara agreed.

"I know the one you mean: Why has Santa Claus taken up gardening?" Katie waited for Jason's answer. When he shook his head she said, "because he likes to hoe, hoe, hoe. Remember that one, Jay?"

"I certainly don't," he said. "But if you don't mind, I think I'll steal it to add to my repertoire. He bit into his hamburger.

"You would." Katie reached for one of his ketchup-drenched french fries. "And I bet you won't even pay me a quarter like your brother."

"I'll ignore that," said Jason, "and ask you to go to the mall with me this afternoon, anyway."

"Well, maybe I'll consider it if you promise to let me look at the sweaters they have on sale at Dennison's," she bargained with a sly smile.

"The problem is, you start looking and then finish looking about two hours later. All I wanted to get was a new pair of running shoes."

"Men are all alike." Katie looked to Sara for support. "My dad hates to go shopping with my mother, too. He can spend hours in the sporting-goods department or even a hardware store but if he gets anywhere near women's clothes he gets a headache, starts sneezing, and I don't know what else. My mom thinks it's all psychological, and so do I," she said, staring accusingly at Jason.

"Hey, don't blame me for your father's headaches!" He threw up his hands defensively. "I promise to try not to get one. Do we have a deal?"

Katie grinned. "Deal."

Sara laughed along with her friends. Katie and Jason always teased each other like this. She wished she felt comfortable enough with Dave to relax and have that kind of fun.

Not that she didn't have fun with Dave. It was just a different kind of fun. But it was the playful, lighthearted give-and-take between people who love and respect each other as equals that Sara missed in her own relationship. But maybe that was just because she and Dave didn't know each other all that well yet. She only wished she really believed that.

"Why don't you come with us?" asked Katie, trying to include Sara in her afternoon plans.

"I'd love to," said Sara, "but I promised to cover another Student Activities Council meeting for Dave after school. He's got to drive his sister to her dance class again."

Actually, Sara was looking forward to the meeting. She didn't tell Katie, but she knew it had a lot to do with the prospect of seeing Chris Forrester again.

She was still confused about her feelings for him. How could she be getting a crush on another guy—if that's what it was—when she was dating Dave? Sara knew half the girls at Stanford High would give their right arm to be going out with Dave Reiner. But *she* was daydreaming about Chris, who was cute and really nice but not exactly a heartthrob. It didn't make sense.

"Didn't you come to school early this morning to tutor Dave for his Spanish test tomorrow?" asked Katie, with a disapproving frown.

"Yes." Sara shrugged. "But he really needed the extra help. And he must have thanked me a thousand times," she added defensively.

"I'll bet," murmured Katie under her breath.

But Sara had heard her. "Why don't you like Dave?" she demanded, hurt that her best friend didn't like her boyfriend.

"Because you're the one who always seems to be doing the giving in your relationship," said Katie honestly. She ignored the warning glance Jason threw her way. "And I never see you anymore, either. Dave monopolizes your time. It's like he's molded you into his personal slave."

"Just because I help him out once in a while doesn't mean I'm his slave," said Sara hotly. Angry tears burned behind her eyelids.

"OK, girls, time out!" Jason whistled. "Sara will go to the mall with us another time," he said firmly to Katie. "And in case you hadn't noticed, the bell rang awhile ago." He nodded toward the half-empty cafeteria.

Katie and Sara smiled at each other across the table.

"I'm sorry," apologized Katie.

"Me, too," said Sara with a sniffle.

"I'll call you tonight," she added a minute later as she and Katie parted in the hall.

Katie waved with one hand, her other arm around Jason's waist.

Sara felt a twinge of loneliness as she watched her friends walk away.

Well, she still had her own Spanish class to get through before the end of the day. She should spend her free period studying the math she didn't get to the night before because it had taken her longer than she had thought it would to prepare notes for her Spanish review with Dave that morning.

Sara sighed. Her life was becoming so complicated. Suddenly one of her mom's favorite quotes popped into her head. "Be careful of what you wish for, because you just might get it." That was really something to think about.

"Hey, Sara, it's good to see you!" Chris smiled broadly as Sara walked into the classroom where the meeting was to be held.

Sara smiled back. She always felt good when she was with Chris. It just seemed natural. She never had to pretend to be somebody she wasn't or to like something she didn't. She felt comfortable and relaxed around him, the way Katie must feel when she's with Jason, Sara suddenly realized.

"How does it feel to be the first-prize winner of the Halloween party?" he asked, his brown eyes twinkling behind his glasses.

Sara tilted her head to the side, taking a really good look at Chris. He really was very good-looking, she decided. Not in the same way Dave was—more like Jimmy Stewart in *Mr. Hobbs Takes a Vacation*, one of her favorite old movies.

"Hey, earth to Sara." Chris grinned, waving his hand in front of her eyes.

Sara blinked, startled out of her thoughts. She hoped Chris didn't notice she was blushing. She was embarrassed to have been caught thinking about him that way.

"I asked how it felt to win the costume contest," he repeated.

"It felt great, but I'm not so sure I deserved it," she said.

"Of course you did. Your costume was terrific. I was even thinking of asking you to sing," he said with a mischievous grin.

"I think you would have regretted that pretty quickly," Sara said, laughing. "My voice is *not* one of my best qualities."

"That's OK, you've got plenty of others." Chris's brown eyes stared into hers, serious now.

Sara looked away quickly, thankful that the other members of the council were filing into the room. She wasn't at all sure how to handle the conversation with Chris. Part of her liked flirting with him, but the other part felt guilty. Dave would never flirt with another girl while he was dating her. He wouldn't hurt her that way, and she shouldn't hurt him.

She took a seat in the front row and concentrated on taking notes for Dave's article. She knew he was counting on her, and she didn't want to leave out any important details. She almost felt as though she had to make up to him for what had just passed between her and Chris.

"I think we unanimously agreed to hold a rummage sale to raise money for our drive to feed the homeless and needy," said Chris. "Should we do it the weekend after Thanksgiving?"

Sara raised her hand. "Maybe we should

have it the weekend before," she suggested. "Lots of people go away for the holiday."

"That's a good point," agreed a girl in the second row. Sara recognized Jennifer from the dance.

"Sara, you did a super job on the decorations for the Halloween dance. Would you mind drawing up some posters for the rummage sale?" asked Chris with a hopeful smile.

Sara nodded. "Sure," she agreed. She was already designing the posters in her mind.

Chris winked at her. "Thanks, Sara."

Sara realized she was grinning from ear to ear. She felt happier and more enthusiastic than she had in a long time. It was good to be involved, and this project really interested her.

Her pencil flew over the notepaper. She was anxious to get all the information Dave might need for his article, and there was so much to include.

She was still writing after the meeting had broken up and the others had left.

"You *are* dedicated." Sara nearly jumped out of her seat. She hadn't realized that she and Chris were the only two people left in the room.

"I guess I got a little carried away," she said, shuffling her papers together nervously.

"I'm not criticizing you, I'm admiring you," said Chris, sliding into the seat beside hers. "I just can't quite figure out what it is you're dedicated to."

"Well, to this fund-raising drive, of course," stammered Sara, too surprised to say anything.

Chris looked doubtful. "Are you sure it's not Dave Reiner you're dedicated to?" he asked. "You are going all out to take notes for an article he's going to get all the credit for."

Sara shook her head, confused. "I never even thought about who was going to get the credit," she said. "I just want to help Dave out, that's all. And I do think you've got a terrific project going here."

"First of all, *we've* got a terrific project. You've contributed more to this whole idea than any of the rest of us. And second of all, you might not have thought about who gets the credit for those articles, but *I* think *you* should get the credit, Sara."

Sara couldn't answer. She felt as though she were drowning in Chris's eyes, the most beautiful eyes she had ever seen. She couldn't force herself to look away, and she didn't want to.

"Sorry, kids. I thought this room was empty."

Sara and Chris moved apart, jolted back to reality with a thud. Mr. Randolph, the head janitor, was standing in the doorway holding a mop and a bucket.

"You two are here awfully late," he said as he began upending chairs onto the desks.

"We were just going, Mr. Randolph." Chris stood up and gathered his books.

Sara scrambled to her feet beside him. "I've really got to run," she said quickly, her tongue tripping over the words.

"I'll drive you home," he offered as she hurried out of the room.

"That's OK, I have a car today. See you," she called over her shoulder, anxious to get away by herself for a while. She needed to think things through. She needed to think about Chris, and she couldn't do that while she was sitting next to him.

She pushed open the heavy side door of the school building and dashed out onto the green lawn. It was an exceptionally beautiful fall day, with picture-book white clouds skimming across a bright blue sky.

Sara didn't realize how far she had walked until she almost tripped over a rock. She found herself in the little patch of woods that separated the high school grounds from the two hundred acres that made up the town park. She had walked past her car in the parking lot long before.

Well, she needed to think things over and here was as good a place as any. She spread her jacket on a pool of yellow leaves under a huge maple tree and sat down, hugging her knees to her chest.

"You know, someone's going to see us if we're not careful, and then you might lose your new girlfriend." Female laughter drifted through the woods. Sara raised her head.

"You know she's not my girlfriend." The familiar voice tore at Sara's heart.

"Well, you certainly give a good imitation of dating her," said the girl, now sounding annoyed.

Sara was frozen. Her arms and legs were paralyzed—she knew she couldn't have moved for anything in the world. She'd still be sitting there when the first snow fell and at the spring thaw.

Julie's and David's voices. They were in the park, just on the other side of a thick row of rhododendron bushes.

"I only went out with her a few times before you and I got together again, and I can assure you, baby, that there is no comparison between the two of you," said Dave. "Sara's just a girl who used to be in my eighth-grade Spanish class. Besides, you know I wanted to take you to the dance, but you had already agreed to go with Kyle."

Sara heard Julie giggle. "Well, from now on I'll only date you," she promised coyly.

"Come on, I'll race you to the tennis courts," said Dave. Sara heard the leaves rustling under their feet.

"First one there serves!" squealed Julie.

Sara lowered her head onto her folded arms and let the hot tears spill down her cheeks. They came faster and faster. There wasn't any point in trying to hold them in. She cried until her throat ached. She had never been so hurt in her life.

Chapter Ten

Sara lunged forward, trying to catch the papers that were blowing out of her notebook. The wind had kicked up, and the notes that she had worked so hard on—the notes that she had taken for Dave—were twirling in the air like falling leaves.

"Ouch!" she exclaimed as she kneeled to gather the papers together. It was the first time she had moved in almost an hour, and her back ached where she'd been leaning against the rough bark of the tree. Her legs were tingling all over with pins and needles.

Sara tucked the papers back into her notebook and stood up. She felt so tired, as if all the energy had drained out of her body, but it was pointless to stay in the woods any longer.

Back in the parking lot, Sara slid behind the wheel of her car and turned the key in the ignition even though she wasn't sure where she wanted to go. She kept replaying the conversation she'd just overheard in her mind. The more she thought about it, the more sick to her stomach she felt.

She knew that she wasn't ready to face her mother, and besides, she was probably still at the office. Katie was at the mall with Jason, and Marsha had her watercolor class. She could find her friends if she tried and she knew they'd be sympathetic, but somehow she wasn't in the mood for the inevitable I-told-you-so's.

They'd been right, though. They'd warned her about Dave, saying that she was changing too much for him, and that he probably wasn't really over Julie. But she'd been too stubborn to listen, too stubborn and too naive.

Dave had been her first real boyfriend—well, at least she had *thought* he was her boyfriend. It looked as if she was wrong about that, too. She had had a crush on him for so long that she hadn't wanted to believe that anything could be less than perfect about him or their relationship. Her feelings for

Chris were a sure sign that she wasn't really happy with Dave, but she'd stifled them.

I'm so humiliated, Sara thought. *I'm such a fool.* She didn't realize she was crying again until she felt tears splash on her hands, which were gripping the steering wheel.

Sara thought she'd been driving aimlessly, turning corners at random, but now with a start she realized that she was down near the shore very close to Dave's house.

She spotted a familiar frame-and-glass building with a bright green-and-white striped awning and pulled up in front of Angelina's Bakery.

She wondered if Maria might be there. Maria had grown up with Dave and knew him quite well. Maybe Maria could help her understand what had gone wrong.

Sara climbed out of her car. She hesitated for a second, not sure that she was doing the right thing. After all, Maria was Dave's friend. Well, she could always just buy a pastry. She pushed open the door to the shop, and the bell jingled overhead.

Maria stood behind the counter, arranging a tray of cookies. She looked up as Sara approached the counter, her eyes revealing her surprise, but her quick smile was warm and friendly.

"Sara, hello. What brings you down here today?" She straightened up and adjusted the waist of her apron.

Sara cleared her throat, hoping she wouldn't burst into tears again.

"I was wondering if I could talk to you for a few minutes," she said awkwardly, looking down at the white-tiled floor.

"Is something wrong?" Maria stepped out from behind the glass counter. "Why don't we sit over here?" she suggested, pulling out a chair for Sara and then taking one out for herself.

When Sara didn't say anything, Maria prompted her. "Does this have something to do with Dave?" she asked gently, tilting her head so that her dark eyes met Sara's.

Sara nodded. "I'm not sure I really should have come here," she said, "but you're the only person I know who knows Dave better than I do. I mean, I don't understand him at all—that's part of my problem."

Maria laughed. "I'm not so sure that anyone really understands Dave," she said. "But I'm glad you did come. I've met several of Dave's girlfriends, and I don't always like them, but you're special," she said with a sincere smile.

Sara smiled, too, taking a deep breath and

beginning to relax. "Thanks," she said. "I like you, too. That's why I wanted to talk to you about what's happened," she confided.

Maria nodded, leaning her elbows on the table and propping her chin in the palms of her hands.

"I guess I was really stupid," Sara began. "But I trusted Dave. I thought he really liked me, when all along he was just using me until he could get back together with his old girlfriend, Julie." Sara swallowed to keep from crying.

"Are you sure that's what's happened?" asked Maria.

Sara described the whole afternoon, from Dave's story about chauffeuring his sister to the conversation in the woods. When she was finished she blew her nose loudly on a paper napkin.

"I'm sorry, Sara," said Maria, reaching out to touch Sara's sleeve. "I know how bad you must feel."

"No, you don't. I don't think that anybody can. I really cared about Dave, and I thought he cared about me. But I was just somebody that tutored him in Spanish and took his notes. He used me as a substitute date for the dance because Julie was going with somebody else." Sara pulled another napkin from the metal dispenser and wiped her eyes.

"Listen to me," Maria insisted firmly. "You have a perfect right to be hurt, but you have a right to be angry, too. Dave treated you badly, but I'm afraid that's just the way he is. He thinks about himself first, last, and always. I don't think he'll ever change."

Sara looked at Maria in surprise.

"I met Julie a few times," Maria went on, "and frankly, I think those two are a perfect match. She's just as self-centered as he is." Maria tossed her head.

"I guess I really should be angry," Sara agreed slowly, hiccuping.

"Of course you should be! Dave and I grew up together, and over all those years we've become friends. Luckily we've never been more than that, and I think that's why we've been able to stay close. But I don't see him through rose-colored glasses the way you did. I see him for what he is: good-looking, intelligent, charming, but sometimes a very selfish person. And you know something, Sara?" asked Maria with a hint of a smile.

Sara shook her head helplessly.

"You're lucky this happened now. What if your relationship with Dave had gone on longer, and *then* something like this had happened? You would have been even more hurt and upset. There are a lot of nice guys out there, Sara. Find someone who really deserves you," advised Maria kindly.

The two girls stood up, and Maria put a hand on Sara's shoulder. "Tell me something," she said. "In your heart, did you really think you and Dave were alike at all? Did you two have very much in common?"

Sara shook her head, feeling foolish. "No, we didn't, I saw that all along. But I sort of pretended that we did."

Maria pressed her lips together in disapproval. "Maybe that was your first mistake. If you do that, sooner or later you start to resent the other person. People don't always share all the same interests, but a good relationship has a lot of give-and-take in it. Most of all, it means respecting each other. I think you gave too much to that relationship, while Dave gave too little."

Sara knew that if she was completely honest with herself, deep down inside she'd been thinking the very same thing. She had tried much harder than Dave did. He had never even followed up on the offer to let her drive his precious Camaro. He had never been sincere with her about anything, she decided sadly.

"Sometimes you might have to go along with somebody else's plans, but then sometimes the other person does that for you. Most of the time, though, you share things together, because sharing makes you both happy. You should never have to pretend to be someone you're not to get a boy to like you." Maria laughed ruefully. "I really gave you a lecture, huh?"

Sara smiled and blew her nose one last time. "You've made me see things so much more clearly," she said gratefully. "When I came here half an hour ago I was really in a fog. Thanks for helping."

"I'm glad I could. I've known a few Daves in my life, too," Maria said. "Now, how about a hot chocolate for the road?" she offered temptingly.

Sara grinned. "That's just what I'm in the mood for."

Sara was surprised that her mother wasn't in the kitchen preparing dinner when she got home. Her dad must have an emergency patient.

She opened the door that led from the front hall of their house to her father's dental office and peeked in. Sure enough, her mother was seated behind the desk, still wearing her white uniform.

"Mom, are you busy?" asked Sara. She hated to disturb her parents when they were working.

Mrs. Grant smiled. "Come on in, honey. Dad's just finishing up in the office." She motioned for Sara to join her. "Mrs. Kramer was eating a piece of fried chicken, and one of her fillings fell out," said Mrs. Grant with a sigh. "You know your father, he'd never turn down a patient. And I guess I'm glad," she added with a proud smile.

Sara studied her mother as if she were seeing her for the first time. Ever since Sara had been a little girl, her parents had worked together. Sara always felt that her mother had given up so much of her own life just to be her dad's secretary. For some reason, that hadn't seemed to Sara like a very worthwhile or important role.

"Mom," she said hesitantly.

Mrs. Grant put down her pen and looked up expectantly. "Is something wrong, honey?"

"Don't you sometimes feel like you gave up a lot in order to work with Daddy? Didn't you have interests of your own?"

Mrs. Grant's brown eyes opened wide. "Of course not, Sara. I love working with your father. I wanted to be a dental nurse because that was what *I* wanted to do." She smiled. "It was just a bonus that your dad was a dentist. What could be better than to do something you love *with* someone you love?"

"I never realized you trained to be a nurse on your own. I always thought you did it just to work with Dad! You're always telling me to share a boy's interests, and I thought that's what you had done," said Sara in surprise.

"Sweetheart, has something happened between you and Dave?" asked Mrs. Grant gently.

Sara nodded. "We broke up, I guess. Dave's going out with someone else."

She didn't have the energy to go through the whole story again, but her mom seemed to understand without an explanation. She nodded thoughtfully. "I had a feeling that your relationship with him might not last," she said.

"How could you know?" Sara looked disbelieving.

Mrs. Grant reached for Sara's hand and squeezed it gently. "Sara, you two were as opposite as night and day."

"For example, you absolutely love dogs, and it was obvious that Dave had no patience for them whatsoever. You're an old-movie buff, and he's into those modern spy thrillers you dislike so much. He loves fishing, and although you did try I don't think it will ever be your favorite sport. To sum it all up, I wouldn't say you two had much in common at all."

"But you always told me to share a boy's interests, and that's all I was trying to do," Sara insisted, still not understanding how she could have gotten everything so mixed up.

"Sara, I didn't mean for you to change your entire personality for someone else. I never meant you to take my words so literally. To have a good relationship you need to have a solid base of things that you share in common, including similar values and goals in life. And I don't think you and Dave had that."

Sara sighed. "I guess you're right, Mom."

"Later on, if there's something special one person enjoys then it's nice if you can both try to enjoy that together. But a groundwork of mutual respect has to be there first."

Sara realized she'd never looked beneath the surface of her mother's words. She'd been too interested in holding on to Dave at any cost. "Boy," she said, "did I blow it!"

Mrs. Grant laughed and smoothed a hand over her daughter's cheek affectionately. "You know, Sara, somebody begins to care about you in the first place for who you are inside, not for who they can turn you into. The best way to find out if a relationship is right is to be yourself and see what happens. No offense, dear, but I have a feeling that if you'd been yourself with Dave from the start you two would never have made it out of the driveway that first day. With or without Abby's encouragement!"

Sara was suddenly very tired. It felt as if an entire week had passed since she got up that morning. All she wanted now was to crawl into bed and curl up under the covers.

"Mom, I'm not very hungry. I think I'm just going to go on up to my room for a while," said Sara, standing and reaching for the door handle.

Mrs. Grant nodded understandingly. "That's fine, honey. I'll be in soon," she promised.

Sara was never so happy to reach the haven of her bedroom. She kicked off her shoes and collapsed across the bed. She fell asleep with one arm draped around Abby's warm, furry neck.

Chapter Eleven

"Well, this is just great. I guess I should have expected to find the two of you together. You must be thrilled to have put one over on me." Dave's blue eyes gleamed coldly as he turned his angry stare first on Sara and then on Chris.

"All right, Dave, this is study hall, and if you don't want to get us all kicked out, you'd better lower your voice and calm down," advised Chris, his own voice steady and even.

Sara had tried her best to avoid Dave ever since she overheard his conversation with Julie on Monday, but now it was Thursday and her luck had finally run out. She had to face him, but at least Chris was there for moral support.

It had been hard for Sara to confide in Chris, but she wanted to start their friendship off with a clean slate, and the only way she knew how to do that was to tell him the truth about everything that had happened between her and Dave. He had been wonderfully sympathetic, so different from Dave, who was always so concerned with his own feelings that he couldn't tune in to anybody else's.

Dave stood over them now, his brows knit together and his fists clenched at his sides. "Oh, sure, it's easy for you to tell me to calm down. You didn't have your by-line stolen by someone you trusted," he said accusingly.

Sara drew in her breath sharply. "How can you even say the word *trusted*?" she demanded. "I was the one who trusted you. But I guess I can't blame you entirely. I was stupid enough to believe your lies. Especially the one about taking your sister to dance class. That was really a good one. You had me convinced—until I overheard you and Julie at your secret rendezvous in the woods." Sara couldn't help sounding a little sarcastic. It almost felt good to be saying something she knew would shock Dave. For once, she was calling the shots.

Dave's face turned white and then red.

"I was going to talk to you about that, Sara," he said, avoiding her eyes.

"And I was going to talk to you about the article," she retorted. "I guess the editor showed you my draft before I had a chance to bring up the subject, kind of like how I found out about you and Julie before you had a chance to tell me."

Chris reached for her hand and held it tightly in his own. Sara knew it was his way of letting her know he was rooting for her, and that she wasn't alone in this. She didn't know how she would have gotten through this scene with Dave without Chris by her side—she really didn't have much practice in theatrics.

"So you wrote the article to get even with me," accused Dave, his voice stiff and formal. "Well, that's great. If stealing my by-line makes you feel any better, then you're welcome to it." He turned on his heel and marched out of the room.

Sara let out a deep breath as the door slammed shut behind him. She didn't realize she was shaking until Chris put his arm around her and drew her close.

"I didn't write that article to get even with Dave," she said, shaking her head. "I did it to

159

prove a point. I didn't want him to take advantage of me anymore, and I wanted him to know it."

"Sara, don't let him get to you. He's really not worth it," Chris said firmly. "If he thinks your writing the newspaper article for the *Star* is on the same level as the wrong he did to you, then that guy's even more warped than I thought. Besides, that article *was* more yours than his. You attended the meeting and you took the notes. All he would have done is string them together and sign his name."

Sara rested her head tentatively against the warmth of Chris's chest. He smelled clean and natural, like soap, a lot different from Dave and his overpowering after-shave. She felt safe and secure with his arm around her—she wished she could stay like that forever.

"And you know something else?" asked Chris suddenly. "The article you wrote is ten times better than any Dave Reiner's ever had printed."

Sara sniffled. "Do you really think so?" she asked, her words muffled against Chris's denim work shirt.

"Of course I do. Believe me, Ken Lerner is a tough editor. He wouldn't put anything in the *Star* unless it was good enough for *The New York Times*."

Sara giggled and tipped her head back to see the teasing gleam in Chris's brown eyes.

"*The New York Times* is probably going a bit too far," she said, "but thanks." The tight feeling in her chest was beginning to ease up. She always felt so comfortable with Chris. She never had to worry about putting on an act so that he'd like her. Right now, for example, her eyes were probably red and not too attractive. She would have had to resort to a Visine and mascara session before Dave would deign to be seen with her. But Chris cared about her for who she really was.

She glanced around the room, glad that there wasn't a teacher assigned to this study hall. The other kids were busy talking or reading. No one was paying any attention to the two of them.

Chris held her hand tightly in his own. He had strong, capable hands. "Do you really want to be a vet?" Sara asked suddenly.

Chris nodded. "Ever since I was about five years old. My mom always used to complain that I was a one-person humane society, bringing home stray dogs and cats. I always wanted to work with animals," he said with a warm smile.

"Me, too," she admitted. "I always dreamed of opening my own kennel," she said. "Someplace really special, where dogs would want to come instead of having to be pulled by their collars. I used to practice with my stuffed animals back when *I* was about five." Looking into Chris's eyes, she knew he'd understand completely.

He nodded. "Well, maybe you'll reconsider and come work for me as my assistant," he suggested with a grin.

"Maybe we can combine our two careers—you can be the vet and I can run the kennel."

It was fun talking with Chris like that. Sara couldn't believe they'd just met a couple of weeks before. She felt as if Chris had melted a block of ice inside her. She used to worry because she didn't have a boyfriend, and now she had every right to be devastated because of what had happened with Dave. But for some reason she didn't feel bad at all—instead she felt more free than ever before in her life.

When the bell rang they were still staring into each other's eyes, talking seriously and sincerely. Sara felt a real physical pain as they parted outside.

Katie put down her bologna sandwich and stared across the table at Sara.

"Is this Chris you're talking about tall, with sandy blond hair and sexy eyes?" she demanded.

Sara nodded. "What are you getting so excited about? I found him—he's mine!"

"And sometimes he wears these adorable wire-rimmed glasses?" Katie continued.

"Right again. Do you really know him?" asked Sara, her eyes scanning the crowded cafeteria for Chris as she speared a forkful of lettuce.

"You know, Sara, you'd be much better off if you'd just listen to me more often." Katie pried open a pink barrette with her teeth. Pinning back a wayward strand of blond hair, she went on, "Do you remember that cousin of Jason's I've been trying to fix you up with?" Her blue eyes gleamed mischievously.

Sara looked suspicious. "Katie, I'm *not* interested in blind dates and I never will be! Don't even *think* about it."

"Well, he wouldn't be a blind date anymore," said Katie. "Jason's cousin is Chris Forrester." She burst out laughing.

"I don't believe it! You've got to be kidding, Katie." Sara bounced in her seat, knocking her friend's arm.

"Hey, watch out! You almost made me spill milk on my new sweater," squealed Katie.

"Why didn't you *tell* me you knew Chris?" demanded Sara. "I can't believe it! The one blind date that would have been great, and I turned you down!"

"How was I supposed to know you knew Chris?" asked Katie. "It's too much of a coincidence that you two met anyway. Wait till we tell Marsha."

"She *would* skip this lunch period to do extra work in the art room. But she'll say that we were destined to be together, or something mystical like that," said Sara, not sure that she didn't believe that herself.

"You know, it could be true," Katie said. "It was definitely in the stars for you two to meet."

"Well, I'm just glad we did," said Sara, breaking into a huge grin as she spotted Jason and Chris heading for their table.

"Don't look now," she whispered, "but we're being invaded by two cute boys."

Katie turned immediately and reached for her compact mirror to apply fresh lipstick.

Jason bent to kiss Katie hello, then straddled the bench seat to sit beside her.

Chris came around to Sara's side of the table. "Is this seat taken?" he asked with a warm smile.

Sara shook her head, feeling her pulse

quicken. "Not until now," she said, happy to see him.

"Everything going OK?" he asked, his expressive brown eyes turning serious as he studied her face.

Sara nodded, realizing that he was referring to Dave.

"Everything's great," she said, meaning it. "I'd really like to join the Student Activities Council if you think that the group would let me," she said.

She knew that Dave might very well be at some of the meetings, covering them for the *Star*, but so what? The only boy who mattered to her was Chris, and Dave's presence wouldn't bother her at all.

"Are you kidding?" asked Chris, his eyes sparkling with enthusiasm. "The group would love to have you! You'll be our star member," he said warmly, reaching for Sara's hand.

Sara couldn't remember when she had been that happy. The warmth of Chris's touch sent tingles running through her body. Her eyes studied his face and lingered on his gentle, expressive mouth. She found herself wondering what it would be like to kiss him, and then felt her cheeks reddening as she realized that he was staring right back at her.

"Sara, I've been wanting to ask you something," he said, squeezing her hand tightly.

Sara nodded, hoping that he was going to ask her for a date.

"I don't know how you feel about old movies, but I love them, especially the classics. There's a Clark Gable film festival at the Cinema on Saturday afternoon, and they're showing *It Happened One Night*. Would you like to go with me?" he asked, his eyes anxious.

Sara couldn't tear her eyes away from him. She was deaf to the din of noise surrounding her and oblivious of the conversation at the table. All she saw was Chris, the most wonderful boy in the world.

"I'd love to go," she said simply, feeling as if she were floating on a cloud of happiness, and wishing that she never had to come back down to earth.

"Great," said Chris, his adorable smile making her heart do flip-flops in her chest.

"It's a great movie," he continued. "I think you'll really like it. I've seen it seven times," he admitted.

Sara giggled. "So have I, but I'd love to see it again."

"Do you like old movies, too?" asked Chris, sounding surprised.

"I'm wild about them," said Sara. "But I didn't know that you did."

"I guess we have a lot to learn about each other," said Chris, looking happy at the prospect.

"I always knew that I should have been a matchmaker," said Katie, breaking into the conversation.

For once Sara agreed with her friend's choice of a date for her, but sometimes it was better to learn things the hard way. All the time she had spent tutoring Dave hadn't really been wasted, she realized, because he had taught her a very valuable lesson in return. She had learned to listen to her own feelings.

If someone truly cares about you, he cares about you for who you really are. And that was the most important lesson in love.

Sweet Dreams

We hope you enjoyed reading this book. All the titles currently available in the Sweet Dreams series are listed at the front of the book. They are all available at your local bookshop or newsagent, though should you find any difficulty in obtaining the books you would like, you can order direct from the publisher, at the address below. Also, if you would like to know more about the series, or would simply like to tell us what you think of the series, write to:

Kim Prior
Sweet Dreams
Transworld Publishers Ltd.
61–63 Uxbridge Road
Ealing
London W5 5SA

To order books, please list the title(s) you would like, and send together with a cheque or postal order made payable to TRANSWORLD PUBLISHERS LTD. Please allow the cost of the book(s) plus postage and packing charges as follows:

All orders up to a total of £5.00: 50p
All orders in excess of £5.00: Free

Please note that payment must be made in pounds sterling; other currencies are unacceptable.

(The above applies to readers in the UK and Republic of Ireland only)

If you live in Australia or New Zealand and would like more information about the series, please write to:

Sally Porter
Sweet Dreams
Transworld Publishers (Aust) Pty Ltd.
15-23 Helles Avenue
Moorebank
N.S.W. 2170
AUSTRALIA

Kiri Martin
Sweet Dreams
c/o Corgi and Bantam Books
New Zealand
Cnr. Moselle and Waipareira Avenues
Henderson
Auckland
NEW ZEALAND

TRUE LOVE! CRUSHES! BREAKUPS! MAKEUPS!

Find out what it's like to be a COUPLE

Ask your bookseller for any titles you have missed:

1 CHANGE OF HEARTS
2 FIRE AND ICE
3 ALONE, TOGETHER
4 MADE FOR EACH OTHER
5 MOVING TOO FAST
6 CRAZY LOVE
7 SWORN ENEMIES
8 MAKING PROMISES
9 BROKEN HEARTS
10 SECRETS
11 MORE THAN FRIENDS
12 BAD LOVE
13 CHANGING PARTNERS
14 PICTURE PERFECT
15 COMING ON STRONG
16 SWEET HEARTS
17 DANCE WITH ME

Coming soon . . .

COUPLES SPECIAL EDITION
SUMMER HEAT!

18 KISS AND RUN